CRAZY LADIES IN CAPES DEBUT

A Cozy Mystery

by

USA Today Bestselling Author

Dani Haviland

Copyright © 2021

Dani Haviland and Chill Out! Books

ISBN 978-1-950592-31-9

All Rights Reserved

Names, places, characters, and incidents are the product of the author's imagination or used fictitiously for the reader's entertainment. Any resemblance to persons living, dead, or fictional, events, business establishments, or locales, is entirely coincidental. No part of this book may be used or reproduced in any manner without written permission from the author except for brief quotations in reviews or critical articles.

(Cover by Michele Hauf)

Description

Louie witnessed a murder... Or did he? Midtown Anchorage is overrun by crime and this group of little old lady activists is ready to do something about it!

***

Come to Anchorage, Alaska in the summertime where a group of concerned silver-haired foxes have a plan to wipe out crime. Will the young people who stumble on their secret society help or hinder them?

Join Louie and Rita from Arlie Undercover and a few others who try to make the world a better place to live...at least their little corner of it.

Dani Haviland is a *USA Today* Bestselling Author
With top-selling books (#10 or higher) in the following categories:

Satire
Parodies
Time Travel
Family Sagas
British Humor
Animal Fiction
Absurdist Fiction
Historical Fiction
Holiday Romance
LGBTQ Mysteries
Fiction Anthologies
Romance Anthologies
Science Fiction Fantasy
Biographies & Memoirs
LGBTQ Science Fiction
Organized Crime Thrillers
Two-Hour Romance Reads
Cultural, Ethnic & Regional Humor
Multicultural & Interracial Romance
Short Story Anthologies & Collections
Black & African American Historical Fiction
Celebrity & Popular Culture Humor
History of Women in the Civil War
United States Drama & Plays
Weddings
And more!

"Touches of humor…lively romance…intricate plot…and lots of action." ***Judge, Writer's Digest Self-Published e-Book Awards about The Great Big Fairy***

Chapter 1

June 1
Chugiak, Alaska

"What are you doing, Louie?" Rita asked, shifting their baby to her other hip.

"Writing a book. Or trying to."

"You can write? Shoot, I didn't know you could even read," she said with a laugh.

"Hey, that's not nice," Louie scolded. "We don't want LuLu to grow up making fun of people. Whether they can or can't read doesn't change their worth."

"Sorry. You're right. Bad joke…Ouch!" Rita said, her remark ending in a yowl. LuLu had grabbed a fistful of Mommy's hair to bring her closer.

Louie looked up at the clock. "Is it my turn to watch her already?" He set down his pencil and reached for his chubby copper-topped daughter, untangling the eighteen-month-old's tight fist from her mother's auburn hair with a practiced dexterity.

"Yes and no. LuLu has been babbling Dada for the last hour, looking out the window for you. I'll tell you, I've really been getting a workout the last six months since she's learned how to walk. Toddler Chasing ought to be an Olympic event."

"Yeah," Louie said. "It's a good thing she has four parents, not just two. Well, sometimes four, depending on work schedules. Speaking of that, when are Jess and Tina returning? I thought their deep undercover sting in trafficking was done last week. I like you and all, and spending time with you two is fine, but I really miss Jess. At least he's still in Alaska somewhere and not working the SeaTac area again."

"Or testifying in D.C. I don't know which is scarier: bad guys with guns, or lawyers and politicians with agendas. I thought that Senate hearing would never end." Rita arched her back and changed her focus. "Enough about that. Tell me about your book."

“You’ll just make fun of me.” He clumsily tried to shut the spiral notebook with his one free hand and dropped it.

Rita swooped over and picked it up. She pivoted in a tight circle, ending with her back to him and his baby-laden arms, trying to sneak a peek at his work in progress.

“Wow. You have beautiful script, Louie. I take back everything I said about you.” She paused a moment and chuckled. “Well, not everything…”

“At first I thought about writing my life story,” he said, engaging her in conversation to keep her from reading. “That was too scary, though. Plus, I didn’t want to piss off my old family… Oops. Bad word. Sorry, LuLu.”

He shifted her to his other hip, freeing up his right hand. “I mean, I didn’t want to let anyone know who I really was. You see,” his voice lowered to a whisper, “I’m in the Witness Protection Program. Using my own name instead of my nickname Lucky and going back to my natural hair and eye color were the easy parts of disappearing in plain sight. No one knew me as Louie. Some of those guys I ratted on like to read crime stories, though. If I wrote my autobiography, they might recognize me and track me down. I gotta be extra careful. LuLu still needs me.”

Louie gave his little girl an extra squeeze as he moved closer to Rita, trying to retrieve his notes while Rita was distracted with his shocking history.

“Witness Protection? Were you a crook? I mean…” She hid the notebook behind her back and squinted at him. “You didn’t kill anyone, did you?”

“Me? No! My mother was involved with a bad dude. He thought I was his kid. They tried for over a year to get pregnant ‘cause he wanted a son real bad. When that didn’t happen, she got fertility checked. The doc said she was fine; it had to be the father who couldn’t make a baby. She liked Alonzo a lot and didn’t want to lose him, even if he was a creep, so decided to trick him. You know something about what happened there though, don’t you? Alonzo De Luca was Carlos’s dad, too. But not really because he was sterile. That’s why Carlos and I are brothers, sort of. Not real brothers because we had different moms *and* dads, but…” Louie leaned forward and whispered, “Alonzo DeLuca,” then stood up again, “thought he sired both of us. He didn’t try to get rid of me when I was a kid 'cause my mom kept my hair dyed black."

"But you have blue eyes. Wasn't he one of those swarthy Italians?"

"Sicilian," Louie corrected, "but yeah. Mom took lots of vacations with me, kept me out of his sight as much as possible, showed me to him when I was asleep at night or napping. 'Yeah, he's your kid,' she said, 'but you don't want him underfoot while you're so busy.' I got my first pair of brown contacts when I was six. I only had to wear them for brief meet and greets, and then Mom and I were back to this villa or that."

"But what about Carlos?"

"Oh, my mom was just DeLuca's girlfriend from high school or something. He married Carlos's mom, so he'd have a legitimate heir. Rosa didn't try to hide his coloring, though. She said it'd change when he got older, I guess. When it didn't, Alonzo tried to get rid of the 'bad blood' of having a redheaded kid. Those attempts started when Carlos was about a year old. De Luca would try something sneaky, so he could say it was an accident. Stuff like trying to throw him off a balcony or push him in front of an oncoming car."

"When he was only one?"

"Well, maybe one-and-a-half. He didn't believe her when she said his hair would turn black, but since he wanted an heir really bad – and I was hardly ever around and illegitimate – he let it slide. Then one of his goons convinced him she was lying or whatever. That's when he got serious about bumping off Carlos. I did what I could to keep my not-my-blood-brother alive and safe without letting him know I was kind of his bodyguard. We weren't at the same place at the same time much, though. My mom being the girlfriend and Rosa being the wife, they never hung out together. De Luca didn't want that."

"I sort of know about Carlos's story after that, Louie. Arlie found out Rosa was the second one – after Charlene – who'd received his anonymous sperm donation. When Rosa was murdered and De Luca sent to jail, Arlie stepped in and took over as parent. He and Charlene fell in love and got married. Now he has both sons, a great wife, and a baby daughter. One big happy family."

"Yeah, well," Louie lunged for his journal and missed again. "I wish *our* big happy family were back together again. Seems like Jess and Tina are together for work more than they are with us. We finally get a duplex so we can all have our own space and bring up LuLu together, and then our significant others are gone half the time. Shoot, you and I are rattling around with *too* much room!"

"Wah, wah, wah," Rita mocked. "What's got into you?"

Louie scowled and shook his head. "Nothing."

"Liar."

"Hey, that's another word I never want our daughter to hear, okay?"

Rita nodded.

"It's just that you have a real job – almost a career – helping Char in her legal aid business. Tina and Jess are full time with being cops and all…"

"Jess is FBI."

"Yeah, that just means he's a cop working for an organization that's a lot bigger and based further away than Anchorage. What I'm trying to say is you all have real jobs. I'm just a stay-at-home dad."

"Louie, you're not 'just a' anything." Rita gave him back his notebook. "Go ahead and write. We'll make it work. My 'Mama' shift will work around your writing. And if you need a proofreader or whatever, let me know. I'd love to read it. But I promise, I'll wait until you're ready to show it to me before I look at it."

"Thanks. Now, what's for dinner?"

"I'm not cooking; you are," Rita said.

"Nuh-uh. I didn't take out any meat to thaw and I'm tired of peanut butter sandwiches and cereal. Hey, I got an idea. Let's go get some Chinese food. There's this place in Spenard that has the best lo mein anywhere. I haven't had any since I got my new identity."

Rita looked down her nose at him, waiting to hear the rest of the story.

"Yeah, well, I guess since the cat's out of the bag, I can tell you. I was sorta supposed to be in another state, but I didn't want to leave Alaska. Arlie said he'd let me stay if I kept out of Anchorage. Most of the old 'family' is in jail, but there are a few of the contractors still around."

"Contractors?" Rita asked. "Oh, do you mean guys who did the dirty work for the family?"

"Yeah, I guess that's a good way to put it. I don't think they'd recognize me if I went into town. But I don't have a car, and Jess's is in the shop. If you'll drive, I'll stay in the car with LuLu. I'm sure you can find the place by yourself, but…"

"But you want to sneak into Anchorage. Arlie's out of town with his family, so no one's going to tattle on you."

"Gee, how'd you get so smart."

"I've been a bit sneaky in the past, too. I hate to say it, but you and I think a lot alike."

***

"Are you ready?" Matilda asked.

The older, petite Asian woman shook her head then looked up at her friend. Nearly seventy-years-old, Matilda worked in her garden every day, shoveled snow all six months of winter, and was a volunteer for at least four different organizations in the Anchorage area. Her hair was nearly white – in sharp contrast to her brown skin – but her back and arms were stronger than most middle-aged men...and a few younger ones.

"I not ready," the small woman in the red silk pants suit said with a smirk of mischief, "because I haven't warmed up." She leaned into a graceful and slow lunge, reaching forward with the finesse of a professional dancer. Then she pivoted in place, her hand slipping through the air, poised, as delicate and smooth as a watercolor still life. She brought both legs together and suddenly kicked out, knocking the petals off the rugosa rose just inches from her partner. "Now I'm ready."

Chapter 2

"Turn right here," Louie said. "And watch for pedestrians."

"Yeah, I know. Tourist season in Anchorage. More hazardous than the Glenn Highway after the first major snowfall." She put the car in park and turned towards him. "So, what do you want me to order for you? You said the lo mein was good. What kind? Pork, chicken…"

"Everything is good. Just ask for a menu, close your eyes, flip it open, and point. Oh, and add hot and sour soup." Louie reached into his pants pocket and pulled out his fifty-dollar bill. "Make sure you bring me the change. I like Lily and all, and I used to be a big tipper, but this is all I have until Jess gets back."

"No worries. We can go Dutch."

"Huh?"

"You buy yours, I'll buy mine."

"Nah, I'm feeling generous – to you, at least. You're saving me a lot of hassle helping me while I write. I'll splurge a little now."

Louie squinted as he checked out the neighborhood for any vehicles he recognized, digging back into his memories of the life he had tried to forget. He sighed in relief then whispered, "I'll stay in the car and wait here by the tax place. That's the restaurant over there. It should only take about ten minutes or less for them to put it all together. Stir fry cooking is fast. And don't forget the fortune cookies."

"Yes, Louie," she replied with a short chuckle at his childlike insistence. "I'll be right back."

Rita threaded her way through the parked cars at the mini-mall to the almost vacant parking lot two buildings away. By the looks, the 'Customer Parking Only' sign was doing a good job of keeping the tourists out.

She pushed through the red doors decorated with carved

gold-colored dragons and waited for her eyes to adjust. Nearly empty, the only patrons in the dimly lit room were seated at two tables, five dark-haired males in their thirties and forties. Rita quickly looked away as one man tried to make eye contact with her.

She fidgeted with her fingernails, pretending she hadn't noticed him, as the hostess approached her with a menu, ready to seat her.

"Oh," Rita said, nodding to the oversize booklet, "I'm not eating in. I'm sort of short on time, so I'd like to order it to go."

The elderly Asian lady smiled broadly and nodded, handing her the plastic-laminated six-page menu. "Everything here good to takeout. No special menu. You tell me what you want, and we get it right away. No extra charge for containers."

Rita set the oversized menu on the counter, squinted her eyes closed, flipped it open, then stabbed at a page, opening one eye to make sure she hadn't selected the drink or dessert menu. She turned it around and said, "That's what I want for one order."

While the hostess wrote it down, Rita repeated the procedure, saw the food she had chosen said spicy, then changed her mind about the selection process. "Just chicken lo mein for the second order. Oh, and two hot and sour soups. To go, of course."

"You remind me of my friend," Lily said. "Lucky chose his meal like that, too."

Rita blanched, then inhaled, trying to rid herself of a guilty look.

Lily saw her unease and smiled like a teacher who'd caught a student cheating. "You and my friend would make happy family," Lily said. "Like Chinese meal with same name but as husband and wife. Maybe a little red-haired daughter for you?"

"No, I don't think so," Rita shook her head with a shudder. "I don't think my girlfriend would like that," she added with a wink.

"Oh?" Lily asked. She realized what she meant and put her

hand in front of her mouth and giggled. "Maybe one man good for two women. You never know." She giggled again and waved in the air. "I be right back with food."

Rita sat on the upholstered bench by the door and stared at the Chinese New Year Calendar, her eyes seeing the years and caricature animals but not comprehending anything. Tingles went up her arms as she felt the man's eyes on her – the one who had tried to get her attention.

She changed her focus and realized she could see his reflection in the glass covering the calendar. His eyes were narrowed as he studied her, his thoughts so loud, they practically screamed, 'Don't I know you from somewhere?'

"Lo mein and hot and sour soup lady?"

Rita turned and saw the hostess with a tall bag in one hand, the other supporting the bottom. "You pay cash or credit card?"

"Oh," Rita said, fumbling in her front pocket for the money Louie had given her. "Cash. Sorry. I was checking out the calendar and didn't hear you."

Lily took the fifty-dollar bill and held it up to the light. "Sorry. I know you nice lady, but there too many phony monies around this year."

"Yeah, well, let's hope neither one of us get any," Rita said with a nervous chuckle as she glanced at the door, eager to leave the dark-haired man's rude and inquisitive stare.

The vintage cash register dinged as it opened, startling Rita. She looked back at Lily who shrugged a silent, 'Sorry,' then said aloud, "I be right back with change. Not enough in drawer yet. Everyone pay credit card today."

Rita turned to face the door, eager to leave but knowing Louie needed the rest of his money.

Screech…

Startled at the raspy sound of metal scraping, Rita jumped and almost dropped the bag of food. Gulping in embarrassment, she looked down as she realized it was the sound of a chair moving across concrete flooring, nothing more.

The sound of a cruel laugh almost made her look up.

Almost.

Flashbacks of times she'd been tested by gang members, sudden loud noises blasted at her to see if she'd flinch. Punches thrown or shots fired to land on the wall inches from her face. It was either be tough or taken advantage of. She concentrated on slowing her breathing, calming her fight or flight reflex to stand up to whatever bully was nearby.

Why now? She had fled that lifestyle years ago.

Rita flinched slightly then realized it was the little hostess's hand on her shoulder, not a man's.

"No worry," the old woman whispered. "He gone. He asshole, but I no can refuse service." She put a short stack of dollars and a small amount of change in Rita's hand and folded her fingers over hers.

"I still say you and Lucky make cute couple." She shook her head and frowned. "But he gone." Lily put her hands in the air and wiggled her fingers. "Poof! One day here, next day gone. That man and his friends still ask if I hear from him. I tell them truth. I no see or hear from him. He gone. I think he dead."

Lily giggled and covered her mouth. "Last part not true. Yes, he gone, but I no think he dead. I think Lucky very clever. And still very lucky."

Rita grimaced at her words and shoved the change in her front pocket. "Thanks for this," and lifted the bag. "Oh," she said and reached into her other pocket. "I forgot the tip. It's not much…"

Lily shook her head and refused the two-dollar tip. "You use it to buy new hair ribbons for your baby girl. Tell her it gift from me."

"How did you know I have a daughter?"

Lily pointed to the small spot of chewed-up cracker drool on her shoulder and the little curly orange hairs next to it. "I make good detective one day, yes?"

Rita chuckled at the old woman who was probably older than

her own grandmother. "Yes, one day. But how did you know she was a girl? It could have been from a son."

"I guess. Fifty-fifty chance I right. Sometimes that enough." Lily opened the door for her patron and stepped outside, looking for the man who had just left. "Coast clear. You okay to go now."

Rita's eyes shifted back to the area where the other men were seated. Their heads were down, looking over the contents of an envelope, papers and photos spread across the table. They weren't interested in her. At least right now. She slipped out and whispered, "Thanks," to Lily.

Louie opened the car door from the inside as Rita approached, the side of his finger to his lips, and a quick nod to the backseat.

Rita understood that LuLu was asleep and handed him the bag of dinner. Louie looked in it, then pawed through the contents, counting the containers. "Where are the cookies?"

"What?"

"The fortune cookies," he whispered harshly. "I have to have a real fortune cookie. Lily makes them special."

Rita rolled her eyes and reached for her seatbelt, ready to drive.

"I'm serious," Louie said, scowling. "Go get them. She'll stay asleep."

"Come on, Louie. I *really, really* don't want to go back."

"*Pretty, pretty* please," Louie asked, changing tactics, using the same doubled modifier format.

Just as she was ready to put the car in gear and leave, Louie pulled out the emotional ace up his sleeve. "I'd go if I could, but do you know what would happen to me if I was found out?"

A low growl thundered from Rita's throat as she fought back the urge to tell him he was playing dirty, then softened to a hard swallow as she recalled the steely gaze of the man in the restaurant. Louie wouldn't have a chance against someone like him. He really must be lucky. Maybe some of it had rubbed off on her.

Rita took a deep breath to compose herself then walked into the restaurant. This time, she shut her eyes for a moment before she opened the door, avoiding the temporary blindness of the lack of light. The little tinkle of a bell above the door frame announced her arrival.

"Back so soon?" Lily asked as she walked up to her, menus clutched close to her embroidered silk Mandarin-style red dress.

"I…um…forgot the cookies. I hear they're very special."

Lily's eyes narrowed. "They just fortune cookies."

"Oh, I heard you made them special. I mean… I thought you made them special," Rita amended.

Lily grinned. Her suspicions were confirmed. Lucky was one of the few people who knew she scripted the little paper notes stuck inside the homemade sugar and flour cookies. This young woman changing her story from 'I heard' to 'I thought' meant she was covering. Good. Lucky wasn't dead.

"I be right back. I give you extra for forgetting. Maybe your daughter old enough to eat cookie now?"

"If I break it up, maybe. We'll see."

Lily headed toward the kitchen, hiding her wide smile. *'We'll see. This lady and Lucky still together. Good. I can get message to him.*

Lily grabbed the small paper sack she'd forgotten to add to the order, then spied the cookie sheet just out of the oven. "Make new ones better." She quickly wrote out two notes with her special lucky numbers on the backs and placed the slips of paper on two of the circular cookies still on the cookie sheet.

"One for baby girl, too." She pulled one of her favorite quotes from her little silk purse and set it on a third cookie. A quick removal with a spatula, then she deftly folded, pinched, and shaped them. She set her oven-warm creations in small to-go cups to keep from getting smashed. "Perfect."

Rita sat as inconspicuously as she could in the foyer, hoping the men absorbed in their planning wouldn't look her way. One man kept looking up, but he was staring at the door, not six feet to the left where she was. He didn't care who was in the restaurant – just who might come in.

"Sorry it take so long," Lily said, handing Rita the bag. "I make one for your baby, too. What her name?"

"LuLu," Rita said before thinking. She swallowed her groan and looked down. *Stop stressing, woman!* "She's not named after family or anything. She just looked like a LuLu. Speaking of her, I need to get back. I told the sitter I'd just be a sec."

Lily started to say goodbye, but she was too late. The young redhaired woman who seemed like she knew Lucky was already gone, faster than a clueless mama would go.

"I got your damned cookies," Rita hissed through the open car door window. "I hope you're happy!"

"Actually," Louie said slowly, looking in the bag, "I am. Ooh! She made these special for us, too."

"What? How can you tell?"

Louie pulled the little cup out and held it up, verifying it didn't have a sauce in it. "She puts them in these to hold their shape if they're fresh. I think she's kinda psychic or a seer or something. She used to say I had more than one life to live. When I told that to the guys – the bad guys I used to be, ahem, involved with – they teased me and said that was because I was going to spend my next life in prison. Shoot! I never thought I'd spend it as a father living with a man and two women. I didn't even know I was gay back then. Well, I knew I was a little queer, but I thought that was normal."

"It is normal, Louie. Maybe not average, but normal. Now, I want to get the heck out of here. I sure hope to hell you're satisfied with this dinner. I'm not coming back to this neighborhood again for nothing!"

Louie reached around and put his seatbelt on as she backed up, nearly hitting a passing car that had been in her blind spot. "Geez, Rita! Watch it. Are you trying to kill us?"

Rita pulled back into the spot and put the car in park. "Maybe you'd better drive," she said and got out of the car, not offering him a chance to refuse.

Looking around to make sure another car wasn't coming, Louie got out and walked around to the driver's side. By the time he opened the door, Rita had scooted over and was already securing her seatbelt. "Let's not talk about it now, okay? Just get us home. Oh, and make sure we aren't followed. Maybe you should take a few back streets, just in case."

"All right," Louie said slowly. He looked at Rita in a new light. She was always tough, determined. Shoot, if he were straight, she'd be a great wife or girlfriend. But he wasn't and neither was she. They were perfect as parents for their little girl, but right now, Rita was the little girl. A very scared little girl.

He opened his mouth, ready to ask what was going on, when she turned around. "Not now, Louie. Please."

"Right. Home but not directly." He turned the opposite direction he should have, making a loop around the block where the Chinese restaurant was. The neighborhood was old. Most of the homes were built before the big earthquake of '64. Overgrown trees, well-trimmed lawns, and big lilac bush hedges separating the tiny homes, painted a serene portrait just a short distance from the huge and smelly Port of Anchorage.

And then he saw it.

***

"There she is. The woman in red. Whack her!" Brutus hissed into his phone.

Zero tugged out the earbud and took three long strides forward. "Ready for this?"

The older Asian woman cowered in fear but kept an eye on her attacker. Just before the baton hit her, she kicked out.

The stunned assailant faltered briefly, then pulled out a handgun.

Pop! Pop!

And down she fell.

The woman in red was taken out. And Brutus had witnessed it.

Chapter 3

Too stunned to speak, Louie watched in horror as an old woman in a bright red silk Chinese-style dress held up her hands to an attacker. The hefty man in a black suit raised some sort of baton or sword over his head and brought it down, inches from her head. The old woman had dodged at the last moment, her fast action a surprise to the attacker and a relief to Louie.

Was that Lily?

Then a quick pop-pop and the woman was down.

Honk! Honk!

"Let's go, Louie. This is a stop sign, not a red light. The coast is clear. Let's get out of here before that Suburban runs us over," Rita said.

Louie looked in his rearview mirror. A dark blue Chevy with an angry driver sporting mirrored sunglasses and a threatening glare faced him. Unknown features, but the grimace familiar. One of the family.

"Come on, Louie," Rita said, smacking him in the shoulder. She turned around in her seat to look at the driver in the vehicle behind her. "He's bigger than both of us put together."

Louie took his foot off the brake and accelerated around the corner, heading toward the industrial district, his old stomping grounds. There were more small alleys and staging areas to hide in than most people knew about.

A few more sharp turns as he braked down the steep road, then Louie pulled to a stop between two triple-stacked forty-foot sea containers. "Let's wait here for a little bit," he said.

"What was that all about? When I said, 'Make sure we aren't followed,' I didn't mean to pull a fast and furious move."

"Huh? Oh, like the movie? Hey, am I Paul Walker or Vin Diesel, because…"

Louie was stopped by the ultimate mean-mama glare.

Yelling wouldn't have been as loud as her eyebrow-furrowed, squinty-eyed version of 'The Look.'

"Oh." He shifted inside his tee shirt, trying to get rid of that familiar and uncomfortable feeling of being on the run. It stopped suddenly and was replaced by a shiver that galloped down his arms, the vision of the recent murder riding the chill's back with spurs on. His gut clenched and the blood drained from his face. Neck weakened, his head bobbled with an impending faint.

Rita watched wordlessly as his change of emotions slowed to freeze frame. When he began to fall forward, she reached over and shoved his shoulder. "Breathe, dummy!"

Louie gulped air, passing out averted. He panted and took a moment to compose himself – hoping he wouldn't start babbling and embarrass himself further – then whispered, "We don't say dummy in this family."

"Yeah, well, we can if we're talking about a ventriloquist's prop. Now will you tell me why you tore off like a mad man? I didn't see a tail on us. I didn't mean for you to find us a place to hide out."

She looked into the backseat again. "She's still asleep. So, tell me, little Paul, why were you driving like a getaway driver? Did you see someone following us because I sure didn't?"

"No, but I did see Lily get shot. I was afraid the murderer would see us and then want to get rid of any witnesses. Or witness if you didn't see it."

"I didn't see anything. Are you high or something? And who's Lily?"

"Hey, you know I don't do any of that stuff, Rita. I'm the perfect dad. And Lily's the hostess at my Chinese restaurant who makes the fortune cookies. When we were at that stop sign, I looked to make sure no one was coming, and there she was – Lily. She had her hands up like she was getting robbed. I couldn't tell if the big guy had a club or sword, but he brought it down on her like he was either going to beat her with it or cut her in two. She moved away at the last millisecond and kicked out, kinda like she was getting him off balance. He stumbled a little, dropped his stick or sword or whatever, and reached in his coat. He was slick: fast and efficient. Kind of a quickdraw shooter."

Louie lifted his hand as if to copy the movement, then shivered and grabbed the steering wheel again. "And then she fell."

"Louie, there wasn't time for all that to happen. I was with you, remember? And there was a car behind us. He would have seen it, too."

"Or he was the guy picking up Lily's murderer," Louie sighed.

"I'd say do you want to go back to the restaurant. I'll make sure Lily's still alive but honestly, I just want to go home. LuLu's going to wake up soon. If someone was killed, you can ask Arlie about it. I know he's on vacation, but he can call in and get the information."

"No," Louie said harshly, then looked back. His loud voice had startled LuLu. Her eyes fluttered open and when she saw him, she smiled, then fell back asleep.

"I'm not supposed to be in Anchorage. He'll be more than pissed if he finds out. You're right. Let's just go home. It'll be on the news tonight or in the morning. I guess I won't be going back for Chinese food again ever. It's too scary."

***

"Got her?"

"Oomph! She's heavier than she looks," the caped woman said, grasping the semi-conscious woman in red under the armpits, tugging her beneath the overgrown lilac bush. "We're clear. They're gone. Let's get out of here, too."

Chapter 4

"Hey, do you wanna drive?" Louie asked. "I know we just switched, but now I'm kinda jumpy." He paused, snorted, and amended his statement. "Scratch that. I'm *real* jumpy."

"If you hadn't asked, I was going to insist," Rita said, unbuckling. "The mind doesn't know if a threat is from a real or imagined source. Fear is fear, no matter what."

"Yeah, and my scare's a little newer than yours. Only a few minutes more but…" Louie paused and shuddered. "Poor Lily."

Rita rolled her eyes at his delusion but decided it was best not to mention it. "Come on. Get out and we'll play Chinese fire drill again."

"Huh?" Louie asked then realized he'd better get out before she changed her mind, no matter what kind of drill it was.

Rita rushed around the other side, opened his door, and waited for him to find the button on the latch. "Hurry, before another car pulls up."

Click!

"Got it!" Louie turned and scooted to get out with the same movement. Leaning too far forward, he lost his balance and fell face-first into Rita's shoulder. All hands and elbows, he fussed and sputtered, trying to untangle her long amber locks from his fists and mouth.

She awkwardly helped him stand upright, then shoved him back with a growl of frustration. Quickly counting to five, she swallowed another grunt of irritation to push past him and climb into the driver's seat. She glanced over her shoulder and checked on the baby. LuLu was still asleep. Then she saw it looming in the rear window. That gawdy, lifted Suburban was pulling up behind them.

There was no doubt in her mind that it was the same one that had been at that intersection of interest – or speculation or hallucination or whatever it was. They had seen it speed away, but it was back. Why? And why were there two big men in the cab now, not one? Could Louie be right? Could there have been mischief and he – or they – were looking to get rid of witnesses?

Rita gasped and started to call Louie's attention to it but changed her mind. Already on edge, he didn't need more fuel for his fear. She had enough for them both.

"What's taking you so long?" Louie joked as she slowed her breathing to compose herself.

She adjusted the seat with jaws clenched and eyes narrowed. His joke had shoved her from terrorized prey to mean mama moose mode. She turned to him, hazel eyes wide with rage. "What's taking me so long?" she repeated with a hiss. "Hmph! Your long legs and overgrown imagination. Keep an eye out for cops. I'm getting us home in record time. Every frickin' one of these stops signs and lights are now 'yield to faster vehicles.' Chugiak, here were come."

Louie didn't reply, focusing his concentration on searching the side roads and on-street parking for police. Two blocks later, he saw it.

Or thought he did.

He turned around and looked behind him, hoping to see her or it again. It was too late, though. "Hey, Rita, can you flip a U-ie? I think I saw something."

"Nope."

"But…"

"We're going home. No stops, pauses, U-ies, or re-dos."

He squinted, trying to get a better look through the dusty haze of the window, ready to beg again, then thought better of it.

Like trying to catch a butterfly on a windy day without a net – the golden-caped crusader he was sure he had seen was gone.

***

"I don't care if you don't like the color. It's the cape we had on hand. Mable said she would try to get the other ones done by this evening unless something came up. Well, it did. And no,

yellow doesn't make you look fat."

Minerva shifted the silken goldenrod covering over her shoulder and scowled. "You don't have to worry about it with your dark skin. Every color reflects on my pale face."

Matilda chuckled. "Be glad it's not blue. You may look a little jaundiced, but at least you don't look like a corpse. Let me know when you see a car. We want to be seen. We can't be famous crimefighters if no one knows it's us taking out the bad guys."

"There's one!" Minerva said, pulling the shroud close to show off the SSS lettering.

"Go! Go! Go!" Matilda said and gave her a quick pat on the back.

And off Minerva toddled, the gimpy gait from her recent knee replacement as unique as she was.

Chapter 5

Home in record time, Rita and Louie ate their take-out meal together in near silence. Even though they lived in separate units of the duplex with their significant others, when one or both of their partners were out of town, the unique family ate and hung out together. Supposedly it was for the benefit of young LuLu, but everyone knew it was good for their mental health, too.

The two parents took turns cutting up small portions of their boxed meals, putting noodles and veggies in their daughter's bright yellow dinner bowl. "Can you see Stuey yet?" Rita asked.

LuLu stuck her pink plastic spoon in the middle of the food and began to dig furiously, flipping the saucy fare over the table and herself, eager to reveal the one-eyed cartoon character pictured on the bottom.

"Hey, that's not how you're supposed to eat, young lady," Louie said, taking the spoon out of her hand. "That's not how Mommy and I do it and neither should you."

Rita grabbed the washcloth she always kept handy at meals and began to clean up the mess, her lips tight, words held back even tighter.

Suddenly Louie blurted out, "I told you I wouldn't go back to Anchorage again if that's what's bothering you. And that's not just to Ping's, either. This is the last time I'm gonna be able to eat the best Chinese food in the world. Please, don't make this meal miserable for me. I really didn't think it would get crazy. And I really did see Lily get shot." He paused and amended his impassioned remark. "Lily or someone who looked just like her."

"Yeah, well, I'm sorry about the silent treatment. It isn't you. Not really. It's because…" Rita got up and rinsed out the cloth in the sink, then came back to give LuLu a more thorough cleaning. "It's because I saw that big Suburban that was at that…that intersection again."

"When? Where? It wasn't here, was it?" Louie asked, rushing to the living room to look out the front window. "I don't see it now."

"No. Not here. That's why I was driving so fast."

"Yeah, I figured you had to have a good reason, running yellow lights and all with our sweetheart in the car. Are you sure it was the same one? I mean, all tricked out and…" Louie paused and grinned sheepishly. "Yeah, you'd know the difference with something as gawdy as that rig. Was the same man still driving?"

"Yeah…"

"What do you mean, 'Yeah…'? What aren't you telling me?"

"There were two people in the front seat when I saw it. Both were big dudes. I couldn't be sure, but the driver looked like a guy I saw at the restaurant."

"Big, dark-haired, and with a sneer that would peel the rind off an orange?"

"Yeah, that's a good description for him. But we got away. If what you saw was real, they don't know who you are or where you live, so let's move on, shall we?"

"I guess. But it still…"

"Oh, and since you bought dinner and there's only one bowl to wash – LuLu's – I'll bathe her. You go work on your novel."

"I don't know if it's a novel or an autobiography. That's what they call it when you're writing your life story, right?"

"Right. But after seeing those guys you used to hang out with – or their friends – I suggest you go totally fiction. You don't want to give clues about who you are and be tracked down."

"Yeah, I have a daughter to help raise."

"Bring up," Rita said. "You raise peas and curtains."

"And that's why I want you to look at my book before I show it to anyone. How'd you get so smart?"

"I paid attention in school. Here," Rita took the bib off the curly-haired cutie covered with bits of noodles and gave it to

Louie. "Would you do the honors and take care of the dinner mess? We have a flotilla of ducks waiting for us."

"No! Wait. Before you go, we need dessert. This is a big deal for her. Her first Chinese fortune cookie."

"You do know that fortune cookies aren't Chinese, right?" Rita asked, switching the baby to a forward-facing position so she could sit down with her.

"Yeah, I heard somewhere that it's an American gimmick. But hey, these are Chinese because they're made by a real Chinese woman. Lily cooks them and makes up the fortunes herself. Plus, the numbers she gives me are always lucky."

"What do you need lucky numbers for? I've never known you to play the lottery."

"Yeah, well, there are other numbers games out there that aren't exactly legal. I don't play those anymore, either." A smile crept up his face and a chuckle escaped.

"What?" Rita asked, grabbing the bag with the cookies from the counter, setting it out of LuLu's reach in the middle of the table.

"That's another one of the reasons they called me Lucky. I used the numbers Lily gave me in those games. We split the winnings. Hey, hand me one of those cookies, would ya?"

Rita lined up the golden-brown baked fare on the table, keeping LuLu's fast grab away from them.

"Let her choose the first one. Maybe she has my luck."

"Maybe she does, and maybe she doesn't," Rita said. "But I'm telling you right now, there's no way on earth I'll let her run numbers or whatever it is you call illegal gambling."

"No worries there because I'm gonna write books and make a million bucks." Louie heard Rita snort and looked up at her scowl. "Well, maybe thousands. But it doesn't make a difference whether I become a millionaire or only make enough to buy you a bike helmet, little one. I'm gonna write books because that's what I want to do."

Rita chuckled again. "That's the smartest thing I've heard

you say in a long time, Louie. As long as you're doing what you want to do and can still house and feed your family, you're rich."

She turned and gave LuLu access to the choo-choo train arrangement of plastic sauce cups of fortune cookies. LuLu immediately grabbed the caboose unit and shoved it into her face. She tore off the lid with her teeth and looked up, her flour and sugar treasure grasped like an apple bobbed from a Halloween party punch bowl.

Louie reached for the cookie, but she dove into her mama's chest, keeping her prize from daddy's thieving hands.

"Here, let me help you get a better bite, Lu." Louie tried again, this time getting a handful of Rita's boob.

"Hey! Watch it, mister!"

"Sorry, sorry, sorry!" he stammered. "I got the cookie, though."

He held up the folded cookie, then broke off a piece. "Here, LuLu. This part is for you. The paper is for me and maybe your mama."

"What are you going to do with the numbers? There isn't a lottery in Alaska."

"Yeah, but Jess and Tina are in Washington right now. They can play the numbers for us down there. I'll tell Jess what mine are when he calls in and you can give yours to Tina. I'll have Jess play LuLu's unless you want…"

He looked up and saw 'the look' again.

"What? The Washington Lottery is legal. I really want to know if she has my luck. If we win, we'll never have to worry about money."

Rita clenched her jaws again, then realized it wasn't luck, Louie, or numbers that were bothering her. She missed Tina. If she were here, she wouldn't be so tense.

Or would she?

Icy chills ran up her arms at the thought of 'it' and them. That creepy Suburban and those big dark-haired dudes who were hanging around Louie's once-favorite restaurant were vivid in her mind.

She turned to Louie and said, "Promise me we'll never go back."

"Huh? What are you talking about? To Washington? Why would I go there – just to play the lottery?" He realized her frustration had turned to fear. "Are you okay?"

"No... or, yes. Shoot! I guess those guys have me spooked more than I want to admit. The driver looked like he might be the guy who was checking me out at the restaurant. I don't know who the passenger was. They looked like they were cousins or brothers. Or maybe it was because they were dressed alike – white shirts and dark jackets, like they were professionals or in the same fraternity."

"Yeah. Both. I mean, all three."

"Huh?"

"Most of those guys are related one way or another, some are only in-laws. And they're professionals, all right. Like in pro crooks. And the same fraternity like in hazing and terrorizing people, not like in going to college or nothin'. I don't think they have enough hours between five of them to graduate high school much less college. Except for their lawyers. I'm sure they all got degrees, but they're hired and not family."

"How do you know all that? And should I be afraid of them?"

"Remember, my mother was the girlfriend of one of the top bad guys. Alonzo and Luca de Luca were brothers. Even though I was supposedly the illegitimate son of Alonzo, I was still considered family. As you can tell from seeing those guys, we don't look alike. Even with contacts and lots of Lady Clairol, I stood out. Plus, I didn't want to do any of the dirty work. The others liked that I wasn't ambitious, so they didn't rat on me when I made myself scarce in tough situations. I talked the old man into letting me be kind of the messenger. I told him he should make use of my throwback looks to my mother's father's side. I could pass paperwork or information on to contractors without looking like I was part of 'the family.' He bought it."

"And yet you're in witness protection now. What happened?" Rita asked, cuddling LuLu close.

Louie shrugged. "I saved Arlie's life and testified against the dude who shot him." He shrugged again. "Can we not talk about it?"

"You have more layers than a baseball, Louie. Sure. You clean up the kitchen, and I'll take care of the kid. Oh, and make sure all the doors are deadbolted, just in case. I don't think anyone followed us, but I'll sleep better if I know Jess's security system is activated."

"Yeah, but can you spend the night here since Tina and Jess are both gone? That is, if you shaved your legs."

"Yeah, yeah, yeah," Rita said, waving off his familiar complaint, then repeated hers. "And I know you didn't eat beans today, so you're okay for tonight, too."

***

Rita bathed LuLu and brought her into the living room so Louie could read her favorite book to her. "And what's this?" he asked.

"Moose!" LuLu said.

"Yes, and it's time for Mrs. Moose and her babies to go to sleep. Give Mama a kiss goodnight. We'll see you in the morning."

"I got this. Keep working," Rita said, taking the baby from him with a nod to the laptop on the kitchen table.

"Night, night, Dada. See you morning," LuLu hollered over her mother's shoulder as she took her away to her room.

Louie picked up the notebook he'd been writing in and set it next to the laptop. "Time to transcribe my notes," he said, then noticed the two cookies in the middle of the table.

Rita walked in as he picked them up. "Yeah, with all the chatter about your past life, we forgot to get our fortunes." She sat down across from him and looked up at the clock. "And it looks like Tina and Jess are working late or they'd have called by now."

"Well, crooks and human traffickers don't stick to a schedule." Louie huffed in frustration then looked up. "I don't mind that they're in law enforcement, but sometimes I wish Tina and Jess were code enforcers or meter maids. Well, not Jess. He'd have to be a meter man or whatever they call them."

"Louie, you forgot. That's what I used to do, too: rescue stolen kids and adults." She shook her head and pursed her lips. "Jess and Tina can call and talk to us, let us know they're okay pretty much anytime they want, give or take an hour. As soon as their assignment is done, they can hop on a plane and come home. Those who've been kidnapped can't do that. Their friends and families don't know if they're dead or alive. Plus, the sex trade kids are brainwashed, told they're not wanted anymore, that they're tainted…"

Louie put his hand up and shook his head. "I know, I know. Can we just be glad we're safe and have family strong enough to help others? Oh, and look at our fortune cookies. I'm ready for something upbeat now that LuLu's asleep."

"She's in bed. Not asleep."

"Close enough for now."

Louie took the two containers of cookies and the one that LuLu's had been in and set them on the table. He covered them with his hands, shuffling them back and forth like the sidewalk hustler he'd been. "Pick one."

"The middle one. Unless it's empty."

He picked it up and grinned. "You're pretty good at this."

"I figured that one had a better chance of being right. So, give me my cookie," she said, hand out flat.

Louie put the cup in her hand and took his. He popped the lid off and snapped his cookie in half. "Oh, these smell so good when they're fresh. They ought to make a candle that smells like them."

"Or you could get her recipe and bake a batch every week." Rita sniffed the cup and smiled.

"If she's still alive…" Louie added somberly.

"Hey," Rita gently touched his shoulder. "We'll watch the news together tonight. If she was shot or – God forbid – killed, there will be something on the news about it. Even an 'incident' downtown will make the ten o'clock report."

He nodded, sniffing back a tear, and pulled the note out of the cookie. "All is not lost. Look on the bright side for joy. 61.416486

"Mine says 'Red is your Lucky color' and the L in Lucky is capitalized. My numbers are 149.4966053. That's a lot of numbers for the lottery. Plus, who uses a decimal point?"

Louie started chuckling. "I guess we don't need a lottery to be rich. We have family. A real family. What more can anyone ask?"

"How about all of us under one roof?" Jess boomed, walking in the front door.

Smack!

Tina slapped him between the shoulder blades and hissed, "Do you see LuLu around? She's probably asleep. If you wake her up, you…" She paused then looked at the others in the room.

"Yeah, he probably did that on purpose," Rita said, coming in to give Tina a big hug and long kiss.

Louie slipped into Jess's arms but bypassed a smooch, instead looking toward LuLu's room. "I guess you'll have to wait until morning to see her. She's been sleeping all night this week. We're hoping it's her new schedule."

"She's pretty much weaned now. She'd rather drink from her sippy cup and eat finger food than nurse. There's so much of the world she wants to see and explore." Rita sniffed. "I have mixed emotions about that."

Tina gave her a squeeze. "That means we can take a mini-vacation and she can stay here with her dads, right?"

"No problem there," Jess said. "I already asked for two months of family leave. Then I get to stay in the Anchorage Bowl for at least six months after that. Personnel looked at my travel expenses for the last two years and decided it would be more economical to use my computer skills remotely. Very remote since I'll work from home for a while."

"Works for me," Louie crowed.

"Me, too," Jess said.

"Me three and her four," Tina said to everyone, then whispered to Rita, "Finally, a honeymoon with just you."

"Honeymoon?" Rita whispered back. "We have to be married first for that. You mean romantic getaway."

"Can't we have both?" Tina asked, her eyes twinkling with mischief.

"Huh? Wait… Are you asking? I mean, yes, if you're asking."

"Dang it, Tina! I wanted to ask Louie first," Jess said.

"Wait," Louie interjected, a frown of confusion wiping out his beaming smile at the surprise arrival. "You just said family leave. They only grant that if the kid's yours biologically or you're married."

Jess grinned at Louie, then winked at Tina. "I guess I did ask him first. Sort of. Is that a yes?"

"Duh!" Louie exclaimed, then lowered his volume. "Yes, that's a yes!"

"Come on, Rita. I'm ready to share a bed. Sleeping single on a hotel queen sucks."

"Yeah, even for a queen it sucks," Jess agreed. "See you tomorrow, Tina. But not too early."

"You got that one right."

***

"What now?" Zero asked, dipping a pretzel into the foam of his beer.

Brutus shrugged, looking up to make sure they were still alone in their end of the bar. "Without a body, we don't get paid. Are you sure you shot her?"

"Of course, I'm sure. You saw it, too. But hey, since the underground already took her corpse, that means we don't have

to chase down that redheaded couple in that beater Ford SUV. Even if they saw our faces, we couldn't be accused of assault much less murder."

"Saw you," Brutus stressed. "I'm just some tourist, lost at the port, checking out the fancy old houses..."

Zero punched his shoulder, knocking him off balance, then stepped back, ready to fight.

"Hey! What was that for?" Brutus asked, not taking the bait. Fighting with your assigned partners was a sure way to lose your job...or worse.

"I thought you said we were in this together. Fifty-fifty. You find the contracts and I do the deeds. You're too much of a wimp to do anything but forge checks."

"Hey, I haven't forged a check in years. No one uses them anymore, Z. Keep up with the trends. Wire transfers, cash apps, and debit cards are where the bucks are now."

"So, you'll take my word for it and introduce me to the big boss? I want a big-ticket contract. This little grudge kill was too easy."

"Yeah, if you pick up the tab tonight, I will. And I don't mean just drinks. I'm ready for the biggest T-bone they got."

"Deal!" Zero said, hoisting his stein in a toast. "Here's to making the big bucks soon."

Chapter 6

Louie awoke swimming in confusion, a mix of heaven and hell: the tantalizing aroma of bacon and the chilly emotional void of an empty bed. He rolled over the bunched-up duvet, pulled on a pair of sweatpants, and opened the bedroom door into a flurry of sunshine and steam.

"Good morning, Sweetie," Jess said. "Sorry, but I'm still on Pacific Time. I've been craving an endless pile of pancakes and bacon for weeks now. Besides, I figured the smell would be a great way to wake up you and LuLu."

"Papa! Dada! Papa! Dada!" LuLu called through the bedroom door. "I'm up!"

"When did she learn that?" Jess said, his hand on the doorknob.

"A new word every day, at least." Louie stepped back and watched Jess pick her up and hold her close, spinning in place.

"My princess!" Jess sang out. "How do you get prettier every time I see you? Is your daddy feeding you beauty greens?"

"Sort of," Louie said. "She discovered avocados were more fun to eat than squish through her fingers."

"I wouldn't give this up for anything," Jess said, snuggling his face under her chin.

"So, I wasn't dreaming?" Louie asked.

"What? You mean about making this legal? It's always been permanent as far as I was concerned." Jess opened his arm out for Louie. "Such a diverse family we have. Two moms, two dads, all getting along so well together."

"And you don't care that I don't have a 'real' job?"

"Louie, you *do* have a real job. You're a full-time dad. Oh, and from what I've overheard, an aspiring author."

"Part time only for now." Louie looked toward the back door, making sure the ladies weren't up and out already. "And

Rita is a lot of help. I think she wants me to succeed, too."

"We all do. Nothing can get in your way with the support team you have. Now, take our precious or cook the bacon, your choice."

"Come to Daddy," Louie said, reaching for LuLu. "Let's you and I set the table while Papa finishes making breakfast."

Louie put her in her booster seat and strapped her in, and then saw it. The fortune ticket from the night before. With all the excitement, he and Rita hadn't read it.

Jess saw him staring at the little slip of paper. Transfixed. "What's the matter? Find a bill we didn't pay?"

"Oh, no. It's LuLu's fortune from last night's Chinese dinner. Here, look at it. Does it make any sense to you?"

"Wow. Personalized and everything. I thought all these came from some bakery in Cleveland with computer-generated numbers and stylized proverbs. 'The sun will rise and set on your treasure.' The numbers are 120-240812." Jess turned the paper over again, making sure he hadn't missed something. "Those can't be lucky numbers. They're jammed together like some sort of access code or coordinates."

"Yeah, I think maybe Lily was trying to tell me something," Louie said, his head low in shame.

"Louie, is this the same Lily who used to feed you lucky numbers back in the day?"

"Um, yeah."

"Did she come to Eagle River to give them to you, or did you go to Anchorage to see her?"

"I didn't see her. Well, maybe I did. I'm not sure."

"Okay, Louie. One question at a time. Did you go to Anchorage?"

"No, I didn't drive to Anchorage," Louie answered, fighting to keep his slight smile of mischief contained.

"I didn't ask if you drove or not. Answer the question, please."

"Yes, I did go to Anchorage. But I never got out of the car."

Words started spilling out as he multitasked, filling LuLu's sippy cup with milk and pulling a clean bib out of the drawer.

"Rita drove because I really, really wanted Chinese food. I know, I know. Eagle River has Hong Kong Delight, but I wanted real Chinese food, not chicken chow mediocre. Who knows how long Pings will be around? I had to tell Rita I was in witness protection, though…"

"What? She knows now?" Jess asked.

"Well, yeah. I mean, she and I have a kid together and all…"

Jess sat down hard on the chair next to LuLu and looked down, trying to contain his rage. A moment later, he blew out his frustration in a big huff. He lifted his chin and looked at Louie, shaking his head.

"Shit! I mean, shoot, Jess. That's not what I mean. Dang it, that wasn't how it went at all. I know I said I'd never throw that in your face, and I'm not. I'm just mentioning it because there's a bond between Rita and me that can't be duplicated. It has nothing to do with how much I love you or even LuLu. It's just I put half the genes into this little girl, and she did the rest. Even if Rita died tomorrow, she'd still be a part of our lives in LuLu. Can't you see that?"

"So, it'd be okay if Tina and I had a kid together?"

"Ew!"

"Get the picture?"

"Well, yeah and no. I mean, I didn't do it on purpose, really. I thought you left me, or I never would have got drunk to numb the pain. You know I'm not a big drinker…"

"Louie, I know the 'two bottles of tequila' story and I get it. I'm just saying I'm a little jealous of Rita at times. Hell, I'm a lot jealous. But that's not the problem. You weren't supposed to tell *anyone* you were a protected witness with a new ID. I only knew because of my FBI agent status and working with Arlie on a joint task force to get the De Lucas under control. Your ex-old man and uncle are still in prison, but that doesn't mean they don't have friends and family on the outside, looking for you. Grudges run long and deep in that family."

"Yeah, tell me about it. They killed my mother."

"Shoot, Louie. I didn't know that." Jess put one hand on Louie's shoulder, offering him a strip of bacon with the other. "Let's start over. No evasive answers, okay?"

"Okay." Louie took a big bite of the bacon and chewed thoroughly, making sure he got the order of events right before he spoke.

"First, Rita drove the three of us into Anchorage."

Louie saw Jess's eyes widen in rage then look to LuLu.

"She was sleepy and fell asleep right away. LuLu, not Rita. Rita was fine. I figured if I did see someone I knew, I could duck down and stay out of sight. That would have been hard to do if I were driving…"

Jess rolled his eyes, grinned slightly, then nodded for him to proceed.

"Rita got the Chinese food but forgot the fortune cookies, so I sent her back. She got spooked by some dude leering at her and was pretty shook up when she got back to the car. So, I told her I'd drive home via the back roads, just in case someone was following us, I mean, her. I saw – or thought I saw – Lily get shot. Now it was me who was real shook up, so Rita took over driving. She thought I was delusional. Just after that, I saw a woman in a yellow cape, like a golden superwoman but with two, maybe three, S's on the back. Rita didn't believe I saw her, either, except I never told her about the letters. But I did see someone get shot. Jess, I think there's a murderer on the loose."

"Back up. If you saw someone get shot, did you call the cops?"

Louie shook his head.

"Why not?"

"Um, by the time Rita looked, the body was gone."

"How long was that?"

"A second or two…" Louie spooned some scrambled eggs out of the warmer and put them in LuLu's bowl, cut them into smaller pieces, then blew on them to cool them down.

"I guess that could be if Lily was only wounded and crawled off. So, tell me about the woman in the cape. Where does she come into this?"

"I don't know."

"Then why did you mention it?"

"Because I'm beginning to wonder if I'm crazy."

Click.

"Hey, guys," Tina called out over the intercom. "Can I come over and see LuLu? I can tell by the *eau d'* bacon you're all awake. I can smell it through the walls."

Jess pushed the button. "Are you complaining, Tina?"

"Nope. I'm asking. That is, unless I have to beg. If so, then I'm begging."

"Come on over. I'll feed you if you clean up."

"Only after I get my fill of snuggles," Tina said. "Be there in a flash with bear bells on."

"Make sure you're wearing more than that."

"Okay, if you insist. It is summer, after all."

"The more skin exposed, the more chance you'll have of mosquito bites. Is Rita coming? I haven't set the table yet."

"Nope, just me for now."

Jiggle, jiggle. Click.

The door opened and Tina walked in, clad in a rainbow-hued tie-dye tank top over a deep-purple sports bra. She hit end on her cell phone, then stuffed it under her bra strap. Jess looked down and saw legs. Lots and lots of legs. "Where are your pants?"

"Two pair are in the dirty clothes, the other is under the covers on the bed. I didn't want to wake Rita. I think I wore her out last night."

"Ew! Too much information," Louie said.

"I have some workout shorts you can borrow," Jess offered. "They have a drawstring, so should cinch up okay."

"Why? This shirt is longer than they are. Besides," she walked over to LuLu and kissed her on the top of the head, distracting her from stabbing her eggs with her plastic fork, "I came to see her. Our little princess doesn't care what I'm wearing."

"We don't either," Louie said. "It's what you're not wearing that's unsettling."

"Hey," she nudged a chair closer to the other side of LuLu, stealing the girl's attention from her daddy, "I'm wearing all the suggested female undergarments, so chill out.".

LuLu dropped her fork and reached out to Tina to be picked up. "Just a sec, little one. Let me untether you for a great big hug. And then Papa has a hearty breakfast for you."

"Daddy does, too," Louie said. "Well, I helped. I mixed up the frozen orange juice." He turned away from the group and grumbled, "I guess I'll just set the table…"

"What's with the sullen attitude, Louie?" Tina kissed LuLu under her chin and made munching noises. She pulled back and asked her, "Is there something wrong with your daddy, Little Lu? Did the sandman forget to give him good dreams last night?"

"Yeah, well, sort of," Louie said then turned to the cabinets for big people cups and plates.

Tina looked at Jess, saw his frown, and knew something was up. "Geez, I thought you two would be over the top happy after the 'Papa's gonna be around more' announcement last night. Is there something I can help with or is it one of those 'Keep your nose out of this, woman' deals?"

"Actually, Tina, you might be able to help. You've spent more time on the streets in Anchorage than I have," Jess said. "At least, in the downtown area. Have you ever seen or heard of a woman in a gold cape with letters on it?"

"Gold, as in shimmery lame or nugget encrusted? And what letters? Scratch those questions. They don't make a difference because I've never seen anyone – male or female – running around town in a cape, with or without monograms. Lots of dudes and ladies in waist-length jackets with dozens of different emblems, but nothing other than black leather or faded denim.

Why?"

"Because I saw a woman wearing one."

"A cape? Okay. What's so weird about that? It is tourist season in Alaska, after all."

"I saw her just a few minutes after I watched a murder. Rita and I were trying to get out of town in a hurry – before those guys in that big ugly Suburban saw us."

"What?" Jess screeched.

LuLu started whimpering and Tina held her close. "Don't worry, Button. Papa's just confused." She kissed the top of her head. "And so am I."

"You never told me about anyone chasing you, Louie."

"Well, I was getting to that. Sort of. I mean, Rita said she saw it in her rearview mirror, and when she described them, well…"

"Well?" Tina prompted. "I'm interested and I don't know what the hell…help is going on."

"Rita said they looked like they were related to the guy who spooked her at Pings, my favorite Chinese restaurant in the world."

"You went into Anchorage, Louie? Shoot, Arlie's gonna be pissed…I mean, peeved, if he finds out."

"Wait," Jess said. "You know about Louie being in Witness Protection?"

"Now I do," Tina answered with a smirk.

"Did you just trick me? No, wait. You did. Rookie mistake."

"Don't worry about it," Tina said. "I figured it had to be something like that. You just confirmed it. Arlie said that under no circumstances was Louie to go into Anchorage. Anywhere else in the state was cool. He knew he couldn't babysit him all the time, so asked me to keep an eye on him when he was out of town. Like now. Man, I'm glad I'm here, but a part of me wishes I was at Disneyland with them instead."

"Well, I'd appreciate it if no one said anything to Arlie. He doesn't need his surrogate brother-in-law or anyone else to stress him or the crew. I told him not to worry about anything, if anything came up, I'd take care of it. I'm standing by my word, too. That means you, sweetheart," he kissed Louie's blushing cheek, "and that redheaded baby mommy are to lay low for the next six months."

"But…but," Tina babbled. "Why are you punishing her? And me! That means we can't go to the movies or even meet for lunch."

"Sorry, Tina. I know it's not fair to you or her, but you don't know the De Luca's like I do." He looked to Louie. "If you want details, ask baby daddy."

"I wish you wouldn't call me that, Jess. I'm just Daddy. And Rita's just Mommy. When you say it the other way, it's like one or both of us were just DNA donors or something."

Jess nodded. "You're right. Sorry."

Before he could lose the emotional intensity of the moment, he looked to Tina. "Now, I'd appreciate it if you helped me out on this. I'll be around a lot more soon, but I still have to spend a lot of time in Anchorage for the next week or two."

Tina huffed. "Yeah, well, we'll have to rely on their honesty and commitment to LuLu. I have to finish up downtown, too. Paperwork I could do remotely, but I also have a whole butt-load of interviews. I can't do that from our living room."

"You could," Louie said, then realized what that meant. "But I'm glad you won't."

"Enough about work and bad guys. Who wants a Mickey Mouse pancake? We may not be able to join Arlie and family, but we can eat those signature triple-puddle 'cakes!"

"Me, me, me!" Louie said.

"Me, me, me!" LuLu said, copying his tone exactly, adding boisterous handclapping to the excitement.

"Me, me, me, too!" Rita said. "Looks like I'm just in time for the good stuff." She pulled out a chair and sat next to Tina, focusing on LuLu so her girlfriend – fiancée, she reminded herself – couldn't see the guilty look on her face. Her timing looked fortunate, but she had delayed her breakfast entrance until the real-life drama of dealing with gangsters and kidnappers had died down. She didn't want to promise anyone anything. Breaking promises sucked for everyone.

***

"Are you okay, Hana?" asked Mabel.

"Oof. Yeah, I guess so. Dang, Zandra really packed a punch," Hana said, rubbing her belly.

"She didn't punch you. She shot you. With a blank. Plus, you were wearing a bullet-proof vest just in case someone swapped guns with her."

"It was two shots, and blank or not, there's a projectile that comes out of that nozzle. It hurt!"

"That's muzzle, not nozzle. At least, you're not dead. Do you think he bought it?"

"Let's hope so. There are so many variables in this, I'm beginning to get scared. Are you sure Winnie knows what she's doing?"

"Hush! Never call Winifred that, even when she's not around. And yes, I'm sure she knows what's she's doing. She's lost so much in her fight against crime. There's no turning back now."

"Well, yeah, there's always turning back," Hana said, unbuttoning her long blouse to remove the Kevlar vest. "It's just sometimes I'm afraid she thinks we're disposable."

"We're soldiers, Hana. We do what we're told. General Winifred has a master plan and we're just the first act in wiping out crime in Alaska."

"Well, at least Anchorage. Alaska is a pretty big property for just a handful of old ladies."

"Experienced females of the warrior persuasion," Mabel said. "Xena and Diana Prince have nothing on us."

Hana snorted and dropped the vest to the floor. "Good. Then next time, you get shot and I'll wear the cape."

Chapter 7

"Hi, may I speak with Lily?" Rita asked.

Louie's hands were flapping in the air, trying to get her attention. She shook her head and turned away, not wanting to be distracted by his animations.

"No, this is her oral hygienist. We have to reschedule her cleaning. Do you know what time she'll be in? Oh? Really? Okay. I'll try this evening, I mean, later on this afternoon. Her appointment isn't until Wednesday. Thank you."

"Ah, man!" Louie groaned, taking the bag of rice away from LuLu's swift hands. "Why didn't you tell me what you were going to ask?"

"I was going to say I was her niece or cousin or something, then realized I didn't have her accent. I was winging it."

"Well, first off, her real name isn't Lily. That's just what I call her because I can't pronounce her real name, the name the guys in back call her. Patrons just refer to her as the hostess."

"Shit."

Louie covered LuLu's ears. "Potty mouth."

"Sorry. So, you're the only one who calls her Lily?"

"Yeah, as far as I know. And another thing, I'm pretty sure she has false teeth. They're extra white and look too big, like she bought them mail order and got the wrong size but wears them anyhow."

"Oh, crap." Rita huffed, then glanced sideways at him. "At least I didn't say the other word."

Louie put his face in LuLu's. "We're going to have to get your mommy to expand her exclamatory vocabulary to include more than fecal matter synonyms, huh?"

"Where'd that come from? I didn't know you knew big words, Louie."

"Hey, I read. Now, you'd better get the heck out of here.

Driving all the way out to the valley to use the phone at Sprawl-Mart was a good idea, but someone's bound to come back to the photo center eventually."

"Yeah, right. Only because we don't need help."

Rita took over the cart driving duty and brought LuLu to the bin of kiddie videos. She pawed through them while Louie looked through the action movie DVDs. He found a gangster shoot-em-up he'd never seen for three dollars and held onto it. "I can't believe I was part of that life."

"Did you ever know anything but that? You told me you grew up in the middle of it."

"Yeah, I guess that's true. But just like this is fiction," he held up the movie, "there were plenty of books and movies about living peacefully – without guns, gambling, extortion, and all that other stuff."

"Quit beating yourself up, Louie. You eventually got where you were meant to be. But, I have to tell you, I'm uncomfortable with all this."

"This what?"

"Sneaking around, trying to find out whether Lily is alive or not. We're not in Anchorage, but we *are* calling your old stomping grounds asking about her."

"Nuh-uh-uh. You're calling, not me. Big difference. Besides, all I said was that 'I' wasn't going there, not you."

"Yeah, well, Tina told Jess she'd keep me away. Pretty much the same thing. Why don't you let it go? Forget about it."

"Rita, have you ever seen anyone killed?"

"No."

"I was there when someone tried to kill Arlie. He almost died in my arms." He shook his head, the memory vivid. "I had his life literally spilling out into my hands. I managed to help a little then, but with Lily, I didn't get the chance."

"First off," Rita said, guiding him away from the two young boys who were trying to eavesdrop on their story, "you helped a lot. Arlie's alive because of you. With Lily, if she were dead for sure, there'd be a body."

Louie shook his head. "No. They have professionals to take care of that. They're called cleaners. They swoop in after a kill and wipe away all traces of evidence. I think that's what happened."

"There wasn't that much time, Louie. I was there, remember? It was not much more than a second."

"Maybe there was a trap door or something and she got away."

"Now you're just making up stuff. You're reading too much fiction, Louie."

"Well, maybe, but maybe not. Hey, I don't think anyone will remember my voice. How about if we go to customer service and see if I can use that phone?"

"No, they're always busy."

"Yeah, you're right." Louie looked at Rita and grinned. "Let's go see what they have in the kiddie department. Maybe today they marked down a bunch of size 2T stuff for clearance."

"You read my mind."

***

"Hey, Boss. Ping's nephew just said someone called here looking for Lily. He knew who she meant, but Lucky De Luca was the only one who called her that. Something smells fishy."

"Yeah, and it ain't the shrimp. But you say it was a broad?"

"Yeah. Somethin' about a dental cleaning or somethin'."

"That old hag didn't have a real tooth in her mouth. I think I'd better send word to the boss that his fake kid might not be dead after all."

"Excuse me," the old woman said, pointing to the table across from the men. "Can you move that chair out of the way for me? I can't get my scooter past it."

"Yeah, yeah, sure," Brutus said. He stood up and she backed away, banging into the bench seat he'd been in.

"Oops!" she said, reaching out to steady herself. "I'm clumsy even when sitting down. Sorry to inconvenience you."

“No problem,” Brutus said with a broad, phony smile. He sat back down and hissed, “Ditzy Dame,” under his breath.

“Hey, that coulda been your mother. Show a little respect,” Luca said. “I’ll send word up the line to Alonzo. You keep looking for that hostess. You can tell Zero no body, no bucks.”

“But don’t we have to get rid of the body if we find it? Zero said he’s one step ahead on this kill. Isn’t it a good thing the old lady hasn’t showed up? No witness, no problem?”

“Eh, doesn’t matter. Dead or alive, I have more cash in my pocket if Zero don’t get paid. Plus, if he’s as good as he claims, he’s probably after your job. If I were you, I’d watch my back.”

Brutus bristled at the thought, then relaxed. Zero popped onto the scene as a free-lancer. No referrals, no contacts. If that punk tried to take his place, he’d undo him as quick as a match flame in a downpour. Poof! Gone and forgotten in two heartbeats.

***

The senior drove her scooter past the men to an empty table and pulled in like she parked there every day. She waved away any assistance from the young hostess. “No, thank you, I’d like a cup of hot tea, please. Oh, and lots of sugar, too.”

The confused dark-haired woman took back the proffered menu. “Just tea?” she asked.

“And sugar. Oh, and a few of those fortune cookies I’ve heard so much about. I understand the numbers in them are very *lucky*.” Winifred raised her eyebrows at the word lucky and studied the waitress, watching for twitches, gasps, or any other sign of recognition.

None.

She reached into the basket of her three-wheeled motorized conveyance and grabbed her purse. Fumbling through the colorful recycled-plastic bag like she was searching, she concentrated on the conversation between the two men. The bug she had planted under their table was coming through loud and clear, directly to the hearing aid in her right ear. She had immediately recognized Alonzo Junior – Boss, as he insisted he be called – the slug who was one clever lawyer away from prison time. The other man was new in town. She'd have to tap into the neighborhood security cameras for an image of him. With a nose like his, it shouldn't take too long to run a screenshot through her database to ID him.

Another sluggo polluting the population. That's all Anchorage needed: more crime. Not on my watch!

"Here you go, ma'am," the server said, setting down the teapot, small cup, and a basket of colorful packages of sweeteners.

Winifred pawed through the woven bowl, then looked up. "Nope. No cookies hidden in here. Did you forget?"

"No, ma'am. No fortune cookies this week. We have custard with plum sauce if you have sweet tooth."

"Oh, I have a sweet tooth, all right," Winifred said with a chuckle. She looked back over her shoulder towards the two men in dark jackets. "I want to get my *lucky* numbers, though. Isn't this the place with custom-made fortune cookies?"

"I don't know. This my first day," the demure young girl said, her head bowed.

"Oh, don't worry about it, sweetheart," Winifred said sincerely. "I'm sure your baker will find the time between potstickers and wontons to put together a few."

The young woman shook her head briskly then leaned down and whispered in Winifred's ear, the one without the hearing aid/receiver. "He doesn't make those. Zumu – I mean, elderly lady who does – they say out on a bender for two days. Ping's nephew say that's why they hire me."

"Zumu?" Winifred whispered, making sure she had the name right.

The girl nodded. She looked around to make sure there were no other employees around, then bent down and whispered, "Zumu doesn't drink. He lie about her. She nice woman. Very responsible. She must be sick, very sick. Or hurt." She shrugged and grinned. "But she tough. She be okay." Her slight smile fell, and she added, "I hope."

Winifred patted her arm and slipped a folded piece of paper into her hand. "If you hear from her, let me know. Tell her I have some lucky numbers for her."

"Who are you?"

"Just tell her that crazy old lady on a ruby-red scooter. She'll know."

***

"Let me try it on," Euphoria said, snatching the gift-wrapped parcel out of Eunice's hands and holding it above her head.

"But I picked it up," she argued, jumping up and trying to grab it.

"Yeah, but if it fits me, it'll fit you, too," the taller and much darker older woman said. "Come on, sis. You can try on the next one, okay?"

"Try it on first, you mean?" the petite, pale-faced granny asked.

"Yeah, yeah, that, too, I guess," her six-foot-tall Samoan 'twin' said. She tore into the carefully wrapped package, ignoring Mabel's perfectly matched pattern and equally spaced pieces of cellophane tape, then stopped.

"Well, what's wrong?" Eunice asked. "You wanted to try it on first."

"But I didn't know it was going to be red. I thought this one was supposed to be purple."

"Nope. Just because Mom always dressed us in different colors to tell us apart, doesn't mean we have to keep it up. You may still like purple, but I'm sick and tired of pink. I asked Mabel to kick it up a hue. From now on, I'm wearing red!"

Euphoria shook out the full-length cape, the color as bright as a summer tomato. "At least the letters are the same on this one. The gold-on-gold of Minerva's cape looks good, but gold on red looks good, too." She handed the cape to her little sister. "Can you imagine how good it's gonna look on purple?"

"It's not the color of the cape that matters but how much fear we're going to strike into bad guys on the street when they see us everywhere they turn."

"Yeah, well, that's what Winifred keeps telling us. Personally, Eunice, I think we'd be further ahead if she figured out how to freeze their bank accounts and mess up their car computers, stranding them on deserted roads after a wild goose chase, without cell phone service or transportation."

"I'm sure she can do that and probably will when she's ready. But first, she wants us to make an impression. We have a debut coming up. As soon as we have all our capes and do our superhero acts – averting fake murders, muggings, and robberies – we can clean up this town. When we have our great reputations established, it will be No more Mister Bad Guys."

"Yeah, but this time, we need a crowd, not just one or two witnesses. The trial run on the vest was a good idea. You never know when there might be real bullets." Euphoria ran one finger over the silky cape, now draped over her sister's shoulders. "I wish I was a spider on the wall, so I could hear if we spooked De Luca or not."

"Leave it to Winifred. Remember, she's a positive genius with anything technical. I don't doubt she already has a bug on a wall near that creep. Have a little faith, Sis. We got this."

Chapter 8

That night

"Hey, Louie," Jess said. "It looks like LuLu's well-baby checkup is tomorrow morning. I know you and Rita usually take her, but how about letting Tina and me do it this time? I only met her doc once and Tina never has."

Louie looked up from his spiral notebook, covering the doodle of a superhero he'd been working on instead of writing. "Oh, yeah. That'd be fine. I'll have more time to kick out this third chapter. I can't speak for Rita, though. She's sort of protective."

"Both of you are overly protective if there is such a thing. We agreed to share the parenting between the four of us. Tina and I want to be a bigger part of LuLu's life. We get meals and playtimes with her, but we want to share the heavy responsibilities, too."

"Yeah, well, she's due for her eighteen-month immunizations, so you'll find out how tough being a parent can be, sitting by, watching someone poke your sweetheart with a needle, making her cry."

"Hey, I know it's for a good reason. I promise to behave. Besides. I'll have my arms full of our darling daughter, so I won't be able to reach out and punch the nurse. Plus, Tina will keep me in line."

"Or try," Louie said with a chuckle.

"Hey, Tina may be small, but she's a spitfire. Fast and clever beats brawny and dumb every time."

Louie gave up on trying to unclog his writer's block and closed his notebook with a huff. He stood up and set it on the dresser. "No peeking, promise?"

"Promise. Our love is big enough for a few secrets. As long as they aren't the kind that will get you killed, right?"

"Is that you saying to keep away from my old haunts?"

"Pretty much," Jess said. He reached out and flipped the light switch. "Come on. It may not be dark, but it is bedtime."

"Daddy and Papa time," Louie said. "I'm glad she's sleeping all night now."

"Me, too."

***

"Did you ask Jess and Tina to take LuLu to her appointment just so you could bug me to take you to Anchorage?" Rita asked.

"No. I promise I didn't. It was his idea. Besides, I didn't know about that caped avenger sighting until the news this morning. He'd already asked to take her to the doctor."

"But didn't you promise Jess you wouldn't go into Anchorage?"

"No, I told him I wouldn't go back to my old haunts. I never hung out much in mid-town, so I figure that doesn't count. Besides, it wasn't just me now. Someone else saw a person dressed up like a superhero, this time chasing down a thief in the Spenard area. Come on, please? I don't have a car, or I'd go by myself."

"What? Do you think we'll see Superman or Wonder Woman, too? That there's some sort of caped crusader convention in town, and if you don't go, you'll miss it?"

"No, but if we go hang out in that neighborhood, I can ask around and see who else saw her or it."

"I'd say it was a her or a him. I don't think there are any 'its' running around, with or without capes."

"Well, they could be robots…" Louie shook his head. "Nah, I saw a limp. It was an old man or old woman."

"Or someone who had been shot…"

"See, now you're imagining things, too, Rita."

"I need to get a real job, Louie. I'm spending too much time with you and that overactive imagination of yours."

"Hey, you have a choice. You could sit around here and file your nails again or drive me to midtown. Besides, they have the best donut shops around. I haven't had a decent apple fritter since WP."

"WP?"

"Witness Protection."

"Fine. Besides, you had me at fritter."

***

"Six apple fritters," Louie said to the lady behind the counter. He turned to Rita. "What do you want?"

"You're going to eat six?"

"Yeah, but not all at once. I only want two now. I'll put the others in the freezer for later, like maybe tomorrow."

Rita scowled at him then smiled wide, suddenly aware of the yeasty, cinnamon aroma with overtures of cocoa and coffee, very happy she'd agreed to come. She turned to the woman in the white apron. "Do you have any of those cream-filled chocolate-covered donuts?"

"We call them Bismarcks," the woman said, "and I was just getting ready to set the last batch out. Do you want to eat them now or should I put them in a bag for you?"

"Go ahead and bag them. Oh, and do you have a plain bag, one without your name on it? I'm sort of being sneaky."

The server looked back and forth between Rita and Louie and grinned at the duo – naughty children in adult bodies. She put their orders in separate white sacks. "You look a little too old to be hiding from your mother, but okay."

Louie handed her a twenty and said, "Keep the change. I'm buying hers, too."

She rang up the order and put the change in the tip jar. "I know where you're coming from. I've been known to sneak fried chicken home. My husband thinks I make the best wings in Alaska. I don't dare let him know it's chicken from the grocery store deli, seasoned with bottled barbecue sauce. We all have our secrets, right?"

Louie rolled his eyes – thinking of all the hiding he'd done because of witness protection – and nodded. "Hey, speaking of secrets," he said. "Did you hear about that robbery that was interrupted by someone wearing a cape?"

"Hear about it?" she said. "Shoot, my next-door neighbor's hairdresser's cousin was the one who was held up! Scared the pants off her. The robber, not the caped crusader."

Rita pulled up a stool at the breakfast counter and opened her bag of donuts. "What did you hear?"

"Yeah," Louie added, standing next to her, his first fritter of the day in hand, ready to take a bite.

"Well, it's no secret that Spenard's a little rough. Lots of cheap motels with people looking to score one way or another. It's scary coming to work in the wee hours, but I've never had a problem. I drive a beater sedan, not worth stealing. Anyhow, I guess it all happened just a few streets over. I didn't see it but…"

Ding. Ding.

"Oops. Sorry. I have another customer," she said. "Nothing more happened than was on the morning news anyhow." She turned her attention to the petite gray-haired lady who had just walked in. "Oh, hi, Minerva. What can I get for you today?"

"Oh, my friends and I are having a concerned citizens meeting today. There are only six of us, but we've put the word out for recruits. Better make it a baker's dozen, just in case a lot of ladies show up. Mix up the varieties, but make sure there's at least one lemon custard-filled in there."

Rita was taking her time, enjoying her donut, her eyes dreamy as she swirled her finger in the Bavarian cream, swiping it from the center to the edges to spread it around for her next bite. Louie had wolfed down his first fritter while standing and decided to sit down to eat his second. He eyed the coffee pot, wishing he hadn't been so generous with his change. A second cup of coffee would make the fritter taste even better. Just as he was deciding whether to ask Rita if she'd spring for coffee, he heard it.

“Do you happen to have any of those little packets of soy sauce?” the old lady customer asked. “You know, like they give you at Chinese restaurants?”

“Soy sauce in a pastry shop?” The server shook her head. “Sorry, Minerva.”

“Dang. I really don’t have the time to stop at the store. Would you believe my friend puts soy sauce on lemon custard donuts? She swears it's imperially delicious.”

Louie’s eyes widened and his heart thumped so hard, he thought it’d bruise a rib. He raised one hand, trying to get the woman’s attention and find his voice at the same time.

The server looked at him. “Yes?”

“Not you, her,” he squeaked, pointing to the senior with his pastry.

“What can I do for you, darling?”

“Um, I have some soy sauce packets in the car.” He nudged Rita and whispered, “Give me your keys.”

Rita took the keys from her front pocket and frowned. One look at the terror in his eyes and she bit off any smart-aleck remark and only said, “Here.”

“Be right back.”

Louie dashed to the car and started digging through the plastic bag they used as for trash. He pawed through it and came up with the three packs he had tossed after their furtive trip to Pings three days earlier. “Aha! Imperially delicious.”

He swiped the packets on his pants, making sure they didn’t look like they’d been fished from the trash. A deep breath for composure, and he was ready. Just as he opened the car door, he had a flash of genius. He fished through the glovebox, found a marker, and drew a smiley face with horns on all three of the packets. If these were going to Lily, she’d know who they were from.

Suddenly, Louie felt powerful. He was and he wasn’t back in the game. He was a good guy now. He could be clever and lucky at the same time.

His stomach turned.

LuLu.

No, he wasn't back in the game. He could, however, let his friend Lily know he was alive. He didn't need or really want her to contact him. Just letting her know he was okay was enough.

It would have to be.

LuLu needed her Daddy. Even if she had Jess and two moms, she still needed him.

And he needed her.

Louie strode into the donut shop, his boisterous attitude now calm and reserved. He was at peace with himself and his decision to be just daddy to his little girl. He didn't need to be clever. Being loved was enough.

"Here you go, Minerva," he said.

"How'd you know my name?"

"That's what she called you when you walked in. Oh, and thanks for organizing concerned citizens. I'd offer to join, but I'm not from around here. I live *far, far* away," he said and winked.

Minerva dropped the soy sauce packets into her purse and picked up the box of donuts. "Thanks. You just made my friend's day and saved me a trip to the store. I don't get around as good as I used to."

Louie held the door for her as she left, eyes wide as she limped away.

Suspicion confirmed. That gimpy gait was unmistakable.

The caped crusader he had seen was a little old lady. This little old lady, Minerva.

***

"I got treats!" Minerva announced to the group. "And I even got soy sauce for your favorite lemon custard donut, Lily."

"Ah," the fatigued woman said. "Imperially delicious."

"Are you all right? You look tired," Minerva said.

Lily shrugged. "It would be nice to sleep in my own bed, not on cot in Winifred's basement, but I be fine. It's hard on my eyes, reading that man's sloppy writing and trying to copy it same way.

I have to get his ledger back before he find it missing. On Mondays, he always goes through it with his chiefs, making sure nobody cheat him. He never know he will be reading from forgery. Numbers all wrong...that he see, though." She nodded. "Yes, I be fine, and he be gone. One way or another, he be gone."

Chapter 9

"Did you see that?" Louie whispered, even though he and Rita were alone in the car, and no one could hear them.

"See what?"

"Her limp."

"Yeah, so what? It looks like she has a bum knee or a bad hip. That's not unusual in old people." Rita opened the bag with the last Bismarck and inhaled.

"Go ahead and eat it. I'll give you one of my fritters tomorrow if you want one. Oh, and her limp. She was moving just like that person wearing that gold cape the other day. I mean, I know lots of people probably have bum hips, but she was kind of cocky in the way she moved. Hey, can a woman be cocky or is that just a guy thing?"

"Hell, if I know. Wait. I think they call it sassy with a woman, but I think any female with a lot of attitude could be referred to as cocky."

"Yeah, well, now that I think about it, she was more sassy than cocky. She looked like she could've been holding a rolling pin, ready to take someone out, but I didn't see one. Now, if it had been a knife or gun… Yeah, she was a sassy old lady, not cocky."

"So, mystery solved, right? No more trips into Anchorage or speculation? What you saw was a little old lady getting her jollies pretending to be Wonder Woman or Captain Marvel or someone like that."

"Nope. You're forgetting one big deal," Louie said. He reached over and scrunched Rita's paper bag closed so she would look up at him and stop fantasizing about how great her Bismarck was going to taste.

She frowned but didn't protest. "What am I forgetting?"

"Lily."

“But she has Lily with her somewhere. Isn’t that what all the soy sauce and imperially delicious nonsense was about?”

“How can we be sure without looking around, scouting out the area, asking questions? Hmm…” Louie’s eyes widened in anticipation of overseeing an investigation like Arlie and his undercover detective team did.

“Come on, dude. In case you forgot, you’re still in hiding. You have to have a little faith that Lily’s in good hands. Matilda looked pretty tough…

“Minerva,” Louie interrupted. “As in nervy old broad, not tilly old woman.”

“What’s tilly?”

“I don’t know. I don’t need to, either. I don’t know a Matilda. Now I won’t ever forget the name of that cocky, sassy, and nervy woman. Minerva. I guess I’ll have to believe Lily’s safe. After all, Minerva was going the extra mile to get her something special for her treat, not scouting out torture implements.”

“Louie, go write a book.” Rita opened the bag, pulled out her Bismarck and took a big bite, then put it back. She smoothed out the wrinkles, folded the top, and tried to make it look neater than it had been. “Your imagination is running overtime again.”

“And so’s your appetite. Save some of that for tomorrow.”

“That’s the plan.”

“Plans can change,” Louie said. “Oh, and just for the record, where did we get these? I don’t know if Jess ever goes to Sterling’s Donut Shop, but if he’s ever been there, he’ll recognize these fritters.”

“Four left, huh?” Rita said, looking over his shoulder at the bag on his lap.

“Yeah, so?”

“I have an idea,” she said slowly, licking her lip.

“Like we get rid of the evidence?”

“You read my mind. Do you want the rest of this, or are you okay with just fritters?”

"Just fritters for me," Louie said. "An apple a day is good for your health, so maybe two, three, or four fritters should be even better."

***

"Are you sure you're not getting the flu?" Jess asked and kissed Louie's forehead, checking for a fever.

"Yeah, it musta been something I ate." Louie rolled onto his side and belched. "Glad that was a dry one…ohh."

"Well, stay in bed or on the couch. Tina just texted me. Rita's feeling ill, too. LuLu fell asleep in the car on the way back from the clinic. The doctor told us not to be surprised if she took a long nap, lost her appetite, and was ready for bed early. I guess it's sandwiches for dinner in both households."

"Yeah, getting immunized always knocks her out. Maybe Rita and I are having sympathy pains."

"Pains?" Jess asked, one eyebrow raised in suspicion.

"Symptoms, I mean."

"Well, if both you and Rita aren't eating dinner, I guess Tina and I get to share another meal. I have lots of bacon left. Maybe she has some of those sprouts she's so fond of and a tomato. A big, fat, BLS and T sounds…"

Jess stopped in mid-sentence, Louie's hand grasping his knee. "Oh, sorry, bud." He patted Louie on the shoulder. "I'll just take my food fantasies next door where they'll be appreciated."

"Yeah, you do that. I'll be here, right where you left me."

Jess rapped on the door and Tina answered.

"I got bacon and bread if you have tomato, mayo, and maybe some sprouts."

"Come on in. Rita's still out of sorts. I take it Louie's the same way?"

"Yup. Personally, I think they went out on a sugar spree and are suffering the consequences. Louie smells different."

"Yeah, Rita, too. Kind of like an apple pie." Tina brought out the cutting board and two plates and Jess set the loaf of bread and bacon container on the counter.

"Probably not apple pie, but if I know Louie – and I do – it was apple fritters. He doesn't have a problem with booze, but he doesn't know when to say enough with those."

"That means they probably indulged together."

Tina and Jess stared at each other wordlessly for a moment, both frozen at remembering another time when Rita and Louie over-consumed, and LuLu was the result. Jess spoke first. "At least it wasn't tequila."

"Yeah, if there are going to be any more babies in this oddball family, let's do it the right way: with turkey basters."

"Tina, you crack me up," Jess said. "Let's get LuLu potty trained before talking about more babies."

An awkward silence followed before Tina spoke up. "Let's keep that between the two of us, okay?"

Jess blushed scarlet, a feeling he hadn't experienced since high school. He nodded, too conflicted to speak up. He noticed the newspaper, opened and folded back to an article someone had been inspecting, little smudges where sticky fingers had been pointing.

"Look at that," he said, glad to have a different subject to talk about.

Tina looked over his shoulder, the ulu she'd used to slice the tomato held up. "What's that?"

"It looks like Spenard has a vigilante, an old woman in a cape chasing off a mugger, rescuing a beauty salon owner."

"Hmph. That's what this town needs."

"What?" Jess asked and pushed her hand away so tomato juice didn't drip on him.

"A whole platoon of crazy ladies in capes. Who knows? It might work. I know I was scared to death of my grandma. Maybe the crooks will be, too."

***

"All right, everyone. Pull up a chair or scooter or whatever, but park it and listen up."

Winifred looked around the room and counted. All six of her

core ladies were here plus at least four recruits. A fifth person was in a motorized wheelchair, stealing glances at the last donut. She used a wooden coffee stirrer to cut the maple-frosted long john in half. She looked around for witnesses, then dropped a napkin over it, hastily palming it toward her, slipping it into her open purse.

Dishonest.

A late-comer walked in, head held high, stomping the ground with her cane, announcing her arrival with the clatter-thud of every awkward step taken, whether she wanted to be noticed or not. The pastry thief saw her and maneuvered her wheelchair aside, revealing a folding chair she had parked in front of.

"Here's a place to sit," she said, turning in her seat, trying to reach back and grab it for her.

"Thanks," the new arrival said. "I got this." Cane-lady used her walking assist as a shepherd's crook and pulled the padded seat towards her.

"Oh, and there's half a maple bar left," donut-lady whispered. "If you want more, I have the other half in my purse."

"Oh, I'll do with just half. I have to watch my figure. Too many donuts make getting around even tougher!"

Winifred changed her first evaluation of the food snatcher. The second one seemed a good candidate, too. Personable, challenged, yet not dissuaded by high odds. Just what she was looking for. Six veterans and six recruits. She may wind up with a Dynamic Dozen after all.

Winifred looked around and made sure everyone was settled or could be. She picked up her smartphone, swiped the screen, tapped twice, and chuckled.

HONK!!

"What was that?" the newbies asked, looking around while the others covered their ears.

"Who has an air horn?" another replied.

"Hush," the veterans whispered.

"Yeah, or she'll do it again," Minerva said, then made the

zipped lips gesture and nodded with a severe frown.

"Now that I have everyone's attention," Winifred said, "I'd like to give you a few basic rules of procedure and make some introductions."

Winifred paused for the minor shuffling and posture shifting as a third of the group of silver-haired ladies fiddled with their hearing aids.

"First off, this is a very private and *secretive*," she stressed, "organization. Anything we say or do within these walls is not shared with anyone. Not husbands, children, grandchildren..."

One woman raised her hand, "Does that include wives or partners, too?"

"Yes," Winifred said, "and hairdressers, shrinks, and massage therapists. If that person – male or female – is not an active member of this group, no sharing names, plans, or past procedures, okay."

"Okays," were mumbled around the room. Winifred held up her smartphone again, and 'shushes' and silence followed.

'Person in charge' attitude nailed and glued in place, Winifred put her phone down and continued her opening spiel. "We are the Spenard Security Society..."

"Sorority," one voice called out timidly.

"Spenard Security Society or Sorority or Symposium," Winifred snapped, frustration coloring her words at having to repeat herself. "The last S isn't as important as our resolve to break up crime in our neighborhood. The SSS on our cape is to mark us as friends of the community, out to stop thefts, defacing of public and personal property, and assaults."

A tall dark woman raised her hand and stood up. "Preferably before they happen," she said.

"I didn't recognize you, Euphoria."

"You didn't? It's me. See, I made sure I was wearing purple. Eunice decided she'd switch from pink to red but see." Euphoria held up her new cape, deep royal purple with a shield on the back with SSS embroidered on it.

"And I have mine, too," Eunice said. Not to be outdone by her 'twin' sister, she held up the bright red satin cape she'd received only moments earlier. She swished it around, trying to find the letters so she could show the group their new logo.

"Both of you sit down," Winifred scolded. "I meant recognized as in given permission to speak. We're following Robert's Rules of Order in here."

"Shouldn't that be Roberta's Rules of Order since we're all women?" the recruit with the wife question asked, her hand held high.

"No. Robert is the last name of the man who wrote the book on maintaining civility in meetings and…" Winifred shifted on her scooter, looking closer at the woman who looked familiar. "What is your name, ma'am? You seem to be very invested in our little local group."

The middle-aged woman in camo cargo pants – much younger than the rest of the group – stood up. "Edna, but you can call me Ed or Eddie. I take it we're not using last names here?"

"Edna? As in Edna Goodfellow?"

"Last names…" Eddie drawled, her face splitting into a grin.

"Edna 'No Last Name Given,' you sure look like one of my star pupils back in my early days of teaching high school."

Nodding with her smile still wide, she acknowledged their relationship. "I prefer Ed or Eddie, though. It sounds tougher. From what I've heard, you could all use a little more toughness. Maybe a former US Marine could provide an extra touch of intimidation."

"Glad to have you on board, Eddie." Winifred's back straightened with pride. *The star pupil from the first civics class she'd ever taught was still as tough as ever. And now with formal training courtesy of the United States Marine Corps, the woman's feisty attitude would be focused and even more useful.*

Chapter 10

June 5
Chugiak, Alaska

Louie swiped open the intercom app on his smartphone. "Hey, Rita."

"Hey, Louie," she answered through the speaker on her wall. "You're supposed to be writing."

"I know, but I need to talk to you. In private."

"This is private, Louie." She bent forward and completed the downward-facing dog yoga position. "Jess and Tina are at work. Only LuLu is here."

"Yeah, I know…" Louie put his phone back in his pocket, opened her kitchen door, and stepped in.

"Geez, woman!" he gasped, turning in place to avoid seeing her naked body. Head down, hands and feet flat on the floor and knees locked, her bottom was stark white and pointed right at him.

"Dammit, Louie!" Shocked, Rita stumbled and fell forward, grabbing the fleecy lap blanket as she rolled to the floor. "We have separate homes for a reason. You have to start respecting other people's privacy."

"I do…" Louie said through the hands covering his face, both eyes shut tight in case that didn't work well enough. "Except maybe not as good as I should with you. Sorry. Can I turn around now?"

"Yeah, watch your daughter while I run into my room and get some clothes on."

Louie waited until he heard the bedroom door close before he turned around. LuLu was on her back, both feet in the air, trying to balance a pink teddy bear on the soles of her feet. "Were you doing yoga, too?"

"Airplane!" she squealed and pushed the stuffed animal back in place as it fell towards her.

"Do you want me to play airplane with you?" he asked.

"Don't you dare. She just ate."

"Oh, she'll be okay…"

"Okay, but if she pukes, you clean up the both of you and the floor."

Louie quickly changed plans and sat on the sofa rather than lay beside LuLu on the floor. "Mommy's right. Let's take a raincheck on that airplane ride."

Rita came back in the room. "Now that you've totally ruined my day, what do you want?"

"Hey, it's only nine in the morning. There are a whole bunch more hours…"

"What? Do you want to ruin those, too, Louie?"

"Yes, I mean, no." Louie leaned forward and covered his face with both hands, elbows on his knees, shoulders slumped. "Man, I don't think there's any way I can unsee that."

"Maybe tequila would help," Rita quipped.

His back straightened and he faced her. "No! You remember what happened…"

Rita laughed out loud, then took it down to a chuckle and finally, a snort.

"You said that on purpose, didn't you?" he asked.

"Of course, I did. It was worth you seeing me naked to watch you pale and freak out." She stopped and remembered how her life had been before that one horrible day two and a half years ago.

She'd just been dumped by her girlfriend, Kitty. Drowning her sorrows in alcohol seemed like a good idea at the time. Hooking up with Louie in the liquor store so they didn't have to drink alone had been a dumb decision. It came to a strange but totally workable conclusion, though – shared parenting of the most precious little girl in the world, LuLu.

It could have been so much worse. Louie was dingy but

loveable and didn't have a mean bone in his tall, scrawny body.

Or Kitty could have come back. How could she have ever been attracted to that vile people user? Kitty – the drug dealer turned human trafficker – baited her with sex to get names and locations of the girls she was helping recover from being used as sex slaves. Thankfully, Kitty was in prison, out of her life for good.

Yes, she'd done what was right. She'd kept the baby and later found a wonderful woman in Tina. Louie got back the man he'd loved for so long, too. One big duplex shared between the five of them, and everyone was happy, living in a unique and unusual but wonderful paradise.

Now if Louie would just learn boundaries!

"So, what did you need this early in the morning? No, scratch that. You're supposed to be writing. Is this another one of your distractions so you don't have to?"

Louie shook his head. "I just can't get that image of Lily being shot out of my head."

"Well, maybe that's a good thing. I mean…" Rita poured a cup of coffee and handed it to him, "better than thinking of me doing yoga in the nude, I suppose."

"Not really. I mean, now I have two things to get out of my head. Dang it, Rita, I have to find out what happened."

"Dang it, Louie," Rita said, using Louie's same inflection, "you made yourself a promise. You said you'd get at least one chapter a week written, maybe two. Last time we talked about it, you didn't even know your topic, much less a title."

"If I could just get that image out of my head…"

"Which one?" Rita asked, then giggled. "Sorry. I couldn't help myself. Hey, there's something that's been bothering me, and I think I just figured it out. Did you see any blood? I know you never mentioned any."

"Nooo," he said slowly, rubbing the stubbly whiskers on his chin to help him concentrate.

"Peek-a-boo!" LuLu squealed, copying his pose.

“No, this is peek-a-boo,” Louie said and covered his eyes. He played a couple rounds of the game, then distracted her with a colorful cloth book and sent her to her mini stuffed chair to read.

“Well?” Rita asked again.

“No, I never saw any b-l-o-o-d.”

“You don’t need to do that, Louie. She doesn’t even know what it is, much less how to spell it. If someone, anyone, was shot at point-blank range, there’d be blood. I’m not an expert, but I guarantee it.”

“Wait! Maybe she was wearing a bulletproof vest.”

“You’re forgetting something, Louie. I saw her just a few minutes earlier at the restaurant. She’s a bitty thing. She was wearing a form-fitting red silk dress, and I promise, there wasn’t a Kevlar vest underneath. Plus, there wasn’t time for her to get to where you saw her, vest up, and then get shot.”

Rita looked back and forth from Louie to the door. “However, if she’d hopped on a motorcycle, she could have made it there, but that’s highly unlikely.”

“Yeah, you’re right.” Louie huffed in defeat. “I need more fritters to help me figure it out. Do you think…”

“I think I’m going to enjoy my morning off with my daughter. There’s no way I’m driving all the way to Anchorage for Sterling’s Donuts.”

“Maybe just to Freddie’s in Eagle River?” Louie pled.

“Nope. You’re just finding excuses not to write, Louie. If it’s not within walking distance, you’ll have to live without whatever it is you’re distracting yourself with. Now, scram.”

Louie picked up LuLu, gave her a couple tickle-kisses on the neck, and said, “Be good to Mommy, okay?”

“Okay,” the toddler said, then opened her book, put it on her head, and started walking in circles.

Rita chuckled. “Yeah, she’s your kid. Even if she can’t figure out how to read it, she’ll find a use for it.”

Louie groaned softly as he left. Hopefully, LuLu had her mother’s smarts, not his. Either way, he still wanted a fritter.

Like a flashlight in the dark, he suddenly remembered the senior center shuttle. He checked the time on his phone, patted his pockets to make sure he had cash, then sprinted down the road, hoping to catch it.

Just as he got to the edge of the parking lot, he saw the van pull away. The shuttle wasn't full. He might have been able to get the driver's attention by waving wildly but didn't try. He was too stunned by who he saw.

Sitting right behind the driver was Minerva.

The gimpy lady from the Anchorage donut shop who had made sure she had soy sauce for her friend's donut was looking right at him – smiling and waving.

And seated behind her was Lily.

Or was it?

***

Ping's Chinese Restaurant

"Where are those potstickers? I ordered them an hour ago. And I want some of that special sauce."

The new hostess sighed. They had only been open for fifteen minutes, and he hadn't been the first customer through the door. There was no way he'd been waiting even twenty minutes "Which sauce, sir?"

"The spicy one. That old toothy hostess always knew what I meant. Hey," young Luca De Luca reached out and stopped the young waitress as she left to check on his potstickers. "Whatever happened to her anyhow, the old lady who was here before you?"

"I didn't ask. They just give me good job at fair wage. I'll check and see if someone else know about special sauce for you."

Jennifer slipped through the swinging doors, stifling curse words as she wiped the feel of his suggestive squeeze off her arm. "Hey, Joe," she said without a trace of Asian accent, "that big dude who always sits in the back and stinks like a cologne counter wants some of that special potsticker sauce. He said Zumu used to bring it to him."

"Oh, that. She just poured soy sauce in a dish, added a dash of seasoned rice vinegar and red pepper flakes, then spit in it and stirred. Don't forget the spit. It gives it that special zing." Joe set a deep dish heaped with the meat-filled fried pastries on the counter. "Better get going on it. He'll send them back if these are cold. He won't pay for the second batch, either."

"Why do we put up with him?" Jennifer asked as she assembled the culinary components of the 'special' sauce.

"Why don't you ask Grandma?"

"Zumu? Well, duh! No one's seen her in nearly a week."

"Exactly. He stiffed her for a bill one too many times and she mouthed off, no cussing or yelling, but it was still too much for him. Next thing you know, she doesn't show up for work. And you know Zumu. She'd be here if she had a hundred and four fever and runny sores."

"Ew. Thanks for the visual, Cuz." Jennifer set the sauce dish in the middle of the potstickers.

"Don't forget the special ingredient…"

She worked her cheeks, squinted in disgust, then spat into the soy sauce mix. Stirring the brown brew with her little finger, she groaned and slipped into her naïve and innocent immigrant persona, hastily wiping her pinky on the extra napkins set on the tray. It was going to be a long shift.

***

"How much do you have done?" Winifred asked. "And do you have a name you go by that's easier to pronounce? I'm sorry, but this old white lady's tongue just won't roll around those syllables."

"My grandchildren call me Zumu. That means grandma. Maybe not good for you. Hmm. Lucky always called me Lily. I like that name. You can call me that, too. Oh, and your answer, I have it all done. Do you think Zandra – I mean, Zero – can sneak in without suspicion?"

"No. Her role in this sting is too sensitive to risk even a remote chance that she'll be caught. Or he'll be caught. It's hard to think of her as a him. I saw her – I mean, him – as I was leaving the restaurant the other day. It was hard not to stare. I truly had to focus on the 'Customer Parking Only' sign."

"Yes, 'Zero' is much motivated," Lily said. "How we getting this back to Little Lardo De Luca's office?"

"Not we. You, my dear and essential cohort, are staying underground. Sorry. I know it's summer and the sun's finally shining and warm at the same time, but I don't want you out to see it until we're done."

"But how we get it back? I not there to sneak it in."

"Yeah, well I'm working on that. I haven't figured it out yet. Desperation drives inspiration, though, and I'm just about there now…desperate."

"Well, when you ready to put it back, here is new ledger. This young De Luca not track details - only three columns. This book almost light enough to be carried on back of sparrow."

"And there's my inspiration, Lily. I developed a drone that can slip under just about anyone's radar. I guess it's time to put it to work."

"Miss Winifred, it not radar you need worry about. It eyes of people."

"Have you ever watched a magic show, Lily?"

"Yes, many, many times."

"I was an amateur magician in my teen years. I made a few bucks playing kiddie birthday parties and Thursday afternoon teas for little old ladies. Hmm. I'm one of those old ladies now… Anyhow, I digress. The whole trick to magic is misdirection. You have the audience looking here." Winifred twirled a ballpoint pen over and between her fingers. "While you're working back here…" and pulled a quarter out from behind Lily's ear.

"But this book is bigger. Much bigger."

"Nah. Not much larger than a snapshot photo frame and only a little thicker. Leave it to me."

Chapter 11

"Are you sure it was her?" Rita asked the breathless father at her doorway.

Louie nodded as he arched his back, trying to catch more air after his sprint home. "Yeah, yeah. And that Donut Lady was there, too. The one I gave the soy sauce to. I think they live at the senior center. Why else would they be leaving on the shuttle from there?"

"Geez, Louie, I don't know. Maybe they live nearby and just catch a ride to the store every once in a while." She leaned forward and looked him in the eyes. "Like you do, genius."

"Hey, I don't like the tone of your voice. You make the word genius sound like a slur. I may not be as smart as some folks, but I know how to adapt. A high IQ doesn't mean you're any more likely to survive tough situations."

"Sorry. You're right. And for the record, I don't claim to have a high IQ. Shoot, I don't even know what it is. As I said, I just paid attention in school. I was a..a..." Rita waved her hand in the air, trying to get rid of bad memories and end the conversation.

"A what? Come on. Spit it out. You'll feel better if you do."

"I was a fatty, all right? Chunky, bad skin, and as awkward as a two-legged stool. I was too fat to participate in sports, still can't sing on key even with a harness, and had a lousy home life. I'd go to school early just to get away. Then I'd stay late at the library to get my homework done and read for the same reason – to escape."

"Geez, Rita." Louie shook his head, eyes wide in amazement. "That's hard to believe. I mean, you're gorgeous and have a great figure, and not just for someone who had a baby a year ago. I mean... Well, maybe having a fat body was an odd sort of blessing."

"What?"

"If you were hot, you'd have been out there getting in trouble. The way you were, you developed your brain instead of getting in trouble with booze or drugs or getting knocked up. Oh, wait. That part happened later, huh?"

Rita huffed and shook her head. "Yeah, you're right. No telling what I would have done. So, back on subject. What are you planning? Because I know you want to find out more about Lily."

"Yeah, I want to go see if she's really alive." He shook his head. "I'm *positive* I saw someone get shot and fall down, but I'm also *positive* I just saw her, that same woman."

"What you just said – the way you said it – means to me that you're not sure it was Lily. It could have been someone who looked like her, maybe."

"Hey, I know all Asians don't look alike any more than all white folks do. Maybe she has a twin. Identical twins mostly look alike. Shoot! Look at Chip and Carlos. They're half-brothers but except for their noses, they could be twins." Louie paused then grinned.

"Okay. I can see you just figured something out. What?"

"Tonight's bingo night. Wanna come play stamp the cards with a bunch of old folks at the senior center? Jess and Tina wanted more time with LuLu. I'll be just down the road, so Jess won't worry about me sneaking off to Anchorage. Plus, this way you can verify I'm not going nuts."

"I'll go, but I can't verify you're not going nuts."

"Huh?"

"No 'going,' Louie. You're already crazy."

***

"Hey, I wanted the aqua one. Here, you're a girl; you get pink."

"No way, José. Just because I'm female doesn't mean pink's my favorite color. Plus, did you know in the old days, pink was considered a masculine color?" Rita said, holding her bingo color dabber behind her back so Louie didn't grab it.

"Huh? No way."

"Yup. Remember, I'm the one who spent so much time in the library. It didn't make me smarter, but I definitely learned more weird and random facts than I'll need for the rest of my life."

The two bickered over the color of their bingo dauber while more community members trickled into the combination cafeteria and civic center. "That's him," one old lady said, nudging her friend. "That man with the red hair is the kind gentleman from the donut shop."

"You mean the one who got the soy sauce for…"

Minerva quickly put her hand over the woman's mouth. "Not a word." She brought her hand down. "You promised."

The petite Asian woman shrugged in embarrassment and mimed zipping her lips. "Sealed like twenty-year-old kimchi. Do not open or it very stinky."

"Yeah, well, twenty-year-old kimchi is only stinky. Letting loose a secret could be fatal."

Louie admitted defeat and took the pink marker. He looked up to find a familiar face in the crowd and beamed with recognition. "Hey, Minerva!" he hollered, waving to her over Rita's head. "I didn't know we lived in the same neighborhood."

"How'd you remember my name?" she asked, not committing to whether she lived here or not.

"Well, you sort of look like a Minerva," he said, a red blush rising.

"Hmph." Her glare at recognizing a lie softened. "You remember me from the donut store, don't you? You have a good memory."

Louie bent toward her, a respectful two feet away, and whispered, "Nervy Minerva."

"Yes, yes, that's me," she said, then looked to her friend. "Oh, and this is Hana. She's new to the neighborhood. She's never played bingo before."

Louie stared at her, his eyes narrowed as he inspected her for similarities with Lily. He felt Rita's nudge and gasped, embarrassed at his rudeness. "I'm sorry, Hana. You look like someone I used to know. Oh, and this is my friend, Rita." He turned to Minerva. "She likes Sterling's Donuts, too. We don't get into Anchorage very often. That's why we were splurging."

"You're never too old or too young for a good piece of sugary fried bread, right?" Minerva said and chuckled.

Clang! Clang!

The milling around the tables picked up speed as the participants – mostly gray-haired and with assorted walking assists – found a place to sit or park their rides.

"Come over here with us," Louie said, pulling out two chairs for the latecomers.

Hana shifted her eyes to Minerva, reflecting her doubt about accepting the invitation.

The glance was ignored by Minerva as she sat down with an audible sigh of relief. "Ah, even as uncomfortable as a hard plastic chair is, at least it's better than standing for this old lady. The doctor may have fixed my knee, but I don't think there's a cure for the wobbly bones in my ancient feet."

Hana opened her mouth to remind her that giving up sweets helped but shut it quickly. Minerva knew that. She was simply filling the air with words to make the others comfortable. Complaining was her favorite topic of conversation. It wasn't sexist, political, and had nothing to do with religion. And because it was 'her' discomfort, she wasn't badmouthing anyone else, and no one could argue with her.

Perfect.

Bingo sheets spread out across the table, Minerva reached into her big purse and pulled out a plastic container of colored daubers. "Help yourself," she said, setting it in front of Louie and Rita.

Louie set his pink marker next to the box and reached in, grabbing a sky blue one. "Ah," he sighed, looking back at Rita.

Hana looked at him, then at Minerva, and grabbed Louie's discarded pink pen. She tested the color on the top of her card and grinned. "Okay if I use?" she asked.

"Yeah, sure…"

"Hush," Minerva said. She turned back to Hana and said, "The first number is B4."

"But before is word, not number," Hana argued.

"I got this," Louie told Minerva. He pointed to Hana's card, showed her the B row, then scrolled down and saw she had a four. "Color it," he said.

"Oh, I get it. This game is easy."

"It gets a little crazy when the pattern has to be a big frame or a little frame or a…"

"Hush," Minerva repeated to the student/teacher pair. "What was that number?" she asked the caller.

The cards and number calling went on, the foursome becoming more comfortable. During the breaks for the winners to verify their numbers and pick out their prizes, Louie worked on getting to know more about Hana.

"So, are you from China?" he asked.

Hana shook her head briskly, her distaste obvious. "My father from Korea but my mother was Japanese. She had come to teach women how to grow crops in poor soil but wind up staying because she fall in love. I am proof of love." She giggled. "My name means flower in Japanese."

Louie noticed the outfit she was wearing. It was similar in fabric – or identical, he couldn't be sure – to what Lily had been wearing when she was killed. "That's pretty. I guess slacks and a shirt are more comfortable than a dress. I mean, I don't know what I'd do if I was told I couldn't wear pants and had to wear a skirt."

"Louie, men wear skirts. They're called kilts. Guys say they're very comfortable." Rita shifted her shoulders and squirmed in her chair. "Personally, I think a big old soft blanket with a slit for my head wouldn't be a bad idea. Great for the winter, and just toss it off in the summer."

"Like the man with no name, right? Yeah, I could go for that." Louie turned back to Hana. "So, you were born in Korea?"

Rita grinned. She knew Louie was leading the new arrival in conversation. She did look a lot like Lily but was younger, her teeth normal size, natural – not store-bought. The pantsuit was definitely the same fabric as Lily's dress. Now that she saw it up close, Rita remembered noticing the beautiful pattern of yellow-stitched dragons and lanterns on the hostess's sleek shift. She also recalled noticing Lily's feet. Her white socks stopped just above her ankles, the thong of the black sandals between her toes stark in contrast to her pale legs. Hana was wearing black slippers that looked like ballet shoes. She looked athletic and moved with grace. Lily had shuffled when she walked.

Hana and Lily probably weren't sisters or even cousins. But they either shared the same seamstress or shopped at the same fabric store. It was easy to see why Louie was confused.

"I'm sorry, I didn't hear you?" Rita replied in embarrassment to Minerva who'd been talking to her.

"Oh, it was nothing. I just wanted to know if you had a picture of that beautiful daughter of yours."

"Sorry, I only brought my driver's license and a few bucks," Rita said.

"Oh, here, I have a bunch of them." Louie pulled out his wallet, bulging with photos, one debit card, an expired driver's license, and a laminated four-leaf clover.

"This is from her first birthday. Her name is LuLu. She's named after me."

"Are you her father?" Minerva asked.

He nodded, smiling wide with pride. "I named her."

"Oh, so Rita's your wife?"

Both Rita and Louie shook their heads and grunted in distaste. "Nah," Louie added. "It was sort of an accident…"

"She doesn't need details," Rita hissed, hoping to shut him up.

“Oh, I know you don’t need to be married to have babies,” Minerva said with a giggle. “I may be old, but I’m not senile.”

Rita shuffled the bingo cards in front of her, trying to duck out of the conversation completely. Louie, though, wasn’t finished showing off his little girl. “See, that’s her other mom and other dad. We have a unique family. We’re not weird or anything like that. We’re both engaged, but not to each other. We live in separate homes and everything. It’s a duplex, so we’re right next door to each other in case someone needs a hand or something.”

“Well,” Minerva said, a sweet and genuine smile on her face, “it sounds like your daughter has the best of all worlds. And two loving moms and dads, to boot. What more can anyone ask?”

Louie looked at her, a blank expression as he thought of an answer to what else he wanted.

“That’s a rhetorical question,” Rita whispered in his ear. He turned and looked at her, confused. “That means ‘just saying.’ She doesn’t expect an answer, just agree with her.”

An embarrassed smile crossed Louie’s face. “You’re right there,” he said, then added quickly, “Although winning the lottery would be nice. Of course, you have to play it to win.”

Two late arrivals approached their table and waited for the conversation to end. One woman was very tall, an older Samoan beauty with a headful of salt and pepper curls pinned up, her bright purple slack suit not needed to announce her presence in the hall.

The other was at her elbow, chin up in solidarity. Her attire was identical in cut to the other’s but was tomato red, her hair pure white and pulled in a tight bun, similar to the other woman’s topknot but much smaller. They didn’t look anything alike, but you could tell they belonged together.

Minerva looked up and acknowledged them. “Euphoria, Eunice, you made it! Come, sit with us. These are my friends, Louie and Rita. We’re introducing Hana to the great American pastime of bingo.”

Everyone at the table scooted aside except Louie who got up

to retrieve two more chairs. “I think we can all fit in. Did you see the grand prize? A hundred bucks!”

“It’s mine,” the smaller of the two new arrivals announced. “I’m claiming it.”

“Too late. I already did,” the taller and darker half of the duo replied sassily.

“When?”

“As soon as I found out what the grand prize was two days ago. You move too slow, Eunice.”

“Now, now, ladies,” Minerva said. “You’re supposed to leave the bickering and sibling one-upmanship at home. Here you are arguing, and you haven’t even been introduced.”

“Which one’s Eunice and which one’s Euphoria?” Louie asked, proud he had remembered the names Minerva had used when greeting them.

Eunice nudged her tall, dark sister. “Folks still can’t tell us apart, even when we wear different colors.”

“Hmph,” Euphoria snorted as she looked to Eunice. “That’s because he doesn’t know Mom’s trick.” She turned to Louie and Rita. “Hi, I’m Euphoria and this is my twin sister, Eunice. Mom always dressed us in different colors so she could tell us apart. I’m always in purple, like the letter ‘r’ in Euphoria. Eunice was always dressed in pink like the ‘n’ in Eunice. Except Eunice being the troublemaker she’s always been, has decided that she’d rather wear red now.”

Euphoria turned back to her smaller sister. “Now folks will get confused because they’ll think you’re Euphoria because it has an ‘r’ in it like red.”

Before the two could start arguing again, Rita raised her hand to get their attention. She felt Minerva’s gentle touch and subtle headshake to tell her, ‘No, don’t say anything.’

It was too late, though.

“Yes?” Euphoria and Eunice intoned at the same time.

“I was just going to say Eunice wears red which is a shorter word. Euphoria and purple are both longer, taller words. I, um, don't know if you knew, but it seems like there's a bit of difference in your height…"

"I guess if we're standing right next to each other, you'd be able to tell. But you're right. Just remember that Eunice wears red, and my name is Euphoria which is lo-onger, as is the word purple."

Minerva breathed an audible sigh of relief while Hana hid a giggle behind her hand.

Everyone was warned when she joined the group about the twins and their sensitivity about appearance. Even though their looks were as different as night and day, their personalities were nearly identical. After a while, people really did get them confused. Or rather, they mixed up their names. The similarity of their unusual names was the true reason for the confusion, but you couldn't convince the non-biological twin sisters of that. They had the same mother and birthday, so they were identical twins. That one or both of them were probably adopted had nothing to do with it.

While Eunice was getting seated, a folded piece of paper slipped out of her pocket. It wasn't until Louie dropped his dauber and bent to retrieve it under the table did he see it. Not knowing whether it was his or not, he opened it and read.

'SSS meet tomorrow, 10 AM @ CSC gym. Getting capes.'

Glad that he was still bent over, he feigned scrambling for the dauber, tapping and rolling it on the linoleum like he'd dropped it again. "Oops!" he grunted and looked at the note again, then refolded it and left it where it was.

"Did I get that last number, Hana?" he asked, sitting up, pretending nothing had happened.

She leaned over his numbered sheet and looked, "Nope. Looks like you have losing ticket."

"Hey, it's not over until someone yells 'bingo,' right?"

"Hush, you two," Rita scolded. "There. You got that one. Listen up or I'll switch cards with you. You're only one number away."

"Yeah, and this is the grand prize game…"

"And the lucky number is B4. Not after, but B4," the caller said.

"Wait. What? Bingo! Bingo-bingo-bingo!" Louie hollered, jumping up with so much enthusiasm, he knocked his chair over.

"All right, calm down. Read back your numbers and let's make sure."

Louie called out his numbers, then looked up. The caller was silent. Frowning. "Well, folks, it looks like one of our youngest players tonight is the big winner. Congratulations, Lucky!"

"I'm Louie, not Lucky," he said, suddenly pale and insecure, his palms so wet, his colored marker slipped out.

Louie looked at the pen on the floor then to the caller. Now frazzled, he didn't know which to tend to first.

"Get up there," Rita urged. "I'll get the pen."

Everyone applauded the lanky redhead as he made his way to the front. A few made jokes, asking if he was buying the first round of drinks or would he pay for his kid's tuition.

"A hundred bucks!" he said, waving the short stack of crumpled five-dollar bills that had been used as entry fees. "Oh, and here." He pulled one fiver out of the stack and handed it to the caller. "I don't know if I'm supposed to tip you but have a cuppa on me."

The caller looked at the woman seated beside him. She shrugged then nodded. "Well, then, I guess it's okay. Thanks!"

Louie strode back to the table, a few cheers and calls about sharing rumbling from the crowd of seniors. "Are we done? I'm ready to play another game."

"It's over," Rita said curtly. "Come on. Let's get out of here."

"Are you all right? You seem a little peeved. I mean, I'm sorry it wasn't you who won, but if it was going to be anyone else here, I'm glad it was me."

"I'm glad it was you, too, Louie. I'm sorry for the sour disposition. Something isn't setting well, and it isn't the weak lemonade. I'll feel better once we're home."

"Oh, let me say goodbye." Louie turned toward the table and saw Hana was looking at the paper that had been on the floor. He swished an embarrassed grin at his deception, then let it grow into a giant smile of farewell. "Goodnight, ladies. Maybe we'll see you next time around."

Minerva waved and said, "Then it'll be my turn to win the jackpot." She noticed Hana wasn't joining in the farewell. She was absorbed in a note. "Hana, say goodbye," she whispered.

"Oh, goodbye," she said. "I still say you very lucky man. Be careful going home."

"You, too," Louie said, then realized he had forgotten to fish for information about whether they lived nearby or at the center. It didn't make a difference. He knew when and where the next meeting of the caped ladies was meeting. He could slip away and eavesdrop. Maybe his luck would continue, and Lily would be there.

***

Minerva sat down next to Hana. "I wrote you a reminder for tomorrow's meeting. I knew you didn't have a smartphone, so you can just put the note on your medicine cabinet. You do still live alone, don't you?"

Hana nodded, then pointed to the words in the note. "What is AM? I forget which is which. Is AM morning and BM night or the other way?"

Minerva stifled a chuckle. "AM is first hour of the day, like in first letter of our alphabet. BM means bowel movement – you know, poop. PM is any time past noon. M for midnight is when it changes back to A. Is that easier to remember?"

Hana giggled behind her hand. "American English is different than what I learned. I'll just ask you. That's easier and less embarrassment."

Chapter 12

The next morning

Louie woke up alone. He froze, momentarily stunned at the loss of his partner's presence, then smelled bacon. Having Jess work from home was going to be glorious.

"Good morning, sweethearts," Louie said when he walked into the kitchen.

LuLu was seated in her highchair, gnawing a toasted bagel. She looked up and said, "Dada, I go pee!"

"What? You have to go pee?" Louie asked.

Jess held him back with a gentle touch, stopping him from taking her out of her seat. "No, she's bragging, not asking. I put her on her potty before she was fully awake, turned on the faucet and…"

"I go pee!"

Louie knelt beside her. "You're getting to be such a big girl! I think Papa and I are going to have to buy you some big girl panties."

Jess started to admit he already had, then realized this was a rite of passage Louie wanted to be a part of, too. Instead, he said, "That sounds like a great incentive. It's Saturday, though, and I don't have to work. I was thinking, why don't we go to the zoo instead of shopping?"

"Yeah! She'll still fit in the backpack. Maybe the tigers will be out." At the word 'tigers,' Louie thought of Hana and the scheduled meeting of the old ladies in capes. It might be his only chance to find out what happened to Lily. "Shoot, Jess. I sort of have a commitment. Can we do it at another time… Or you can take all the girls. I don't know if Tina's ever been to the zoo here."

"Actually, she's never been to any zoo." Jess saw the startled look on Louie's face. "Hey, we spend a lot of time together on stakeouts or looking over acres of mug shots. I probably know more about her than Rita does."

"Don't tell Rita that," Louie said and chuffed.

"Don't tell me what?" Rita asked, startling him with her sudden appearance.

"Hey, you're supposed to knock," Louie scolded. "Boundaries, remember?"

"The door was open."

"I had it cracked," Jess admitted. "I had to let out smoke from the first batch of bacon. Come on in. We were just talking about going to the zoo. I guess Louie won't be going. I'm pretty sure Tina said she's never been to the one in Anchorage."

"Never been to any zoo," Tina said, popping in from behind Rita. "And yes, I'd love to go. Rita said she has some sort of interview about a job or something at ten. She has to go into Eagle River for it. So much for pulling weeds and clearing out a space for a garden."

Louie's eyes narrowed in suspicion as he watched Rita for signs of guilt. None. She was good at hiding her emotions, though. She had never mentioned any interviews to him. Besides, who has them on a Saturday? She must have found and read Hana's note when she picked up his dauber. Well, he could be just as sly. There was a whole row of windows at the senior center's gym. He had a fifty-fifty chance of not being on the same end if she showed up.

"Are you sure you don't want to go with us, Louie?" Jess asked.

"I'm sure that I do, but I made a promise to myself to get at least two chapters written every week. If I don't do it today, I'll have to do it tomorrow. There's a practice baseball game down at the park then, and I want to take LuLu to it. If she gets bored, we can always play on the swings."

"I don't know who loves the swings more," Jess said, "you

or her."

Louie started to say, 'She's just like her daddy,' then noticed Jess bite his bottom lip at the implied comparison, that unspoken but apparent jealousy of not being the bio-parent of his little girl showing with his sudden insecurity.

Jess was jolted out of his funk by a sudden, sharp nudge from Tina. "Toss ya for who gets to tote the kid first," she said, a mischievous gleam in her eye.

"And by that smirk, I'll bet you're not talking about flipping coins," Jess said, one arm out and foot forward in a wrestling stance.

"Hey, hey, hey," Louie said. "No partner tossing in the kitchen. If you're gonna do that, you have to go outside."

"I'll tell you what," Jess said. "I'll be a gentleman and let her go first…"

"Grr."

Jess wrapped his arm across her shoulder and whispered, "I only said that to rile you. The first part of the zoo is tough and uphill. It's all easy and level after that. Your choice."

"Okay, I'll go first and ignore that gentleman remark this time. I still say winning first carry with a *real* toss would have been more fun."

"What have you been feeding her, Rita? She's all riled up."

"I'll never tell." Rita sassed, then suddenly changed attitudes from perky to concerned. *I'm sure Louie knows about the meeting at ten. Should I let him know I do, too? If I leave early, I can grab the baby monitor from LuLu's room and hide it in the gym. I won't even have to be there for the meeting to find out what's going on. Just sit back and listen in on my smartphone while relaxing in the woods behind the center.*

Rita's mood lifted with having a plan. "Hey, everyone, I'm going to pass on breakfast and just grab a coffee. I need to go pick up something for my interview. I'll be back in forty."

"Don't worry about it," Tina said. "I'll eat your share of bacon."

"And Louie will eat your pancakes. I think LuLu's already claimed the eggs. We can't keep enough of them in the house."

Rita gave Tina a quick buss, then threw an exaggerated good-bye kiss to LuLu. "Um-mwa!"

"I go pee!" LuLu exclaimed.

"You have to go pee?" Rita asked, lunging to get her out of the highchair to take her to the bathroom.

Louie and Jess interceded. "She went pee by herself this morning," Jess bragged. "No wet diaper. She's a big girl now."

Rita's heart sank with an unexpected despair. The baby she never wanted then wanted so badly was growing up. The hollow feeling was new and horrible.

"Hey, I'd better get going," she said, trying to cover the glum with feigned excitement about the fake job she really wasn't applying for. "Don't wait for me to come back before taking off for the zoo. Crowds start early on the weekend."

Jess looked at Tina and saw the concern in her eyes. They both looked at Louie who was oblivious, playing airplane with the remnants of LuLu's bagel. Either he knew something about Rita's jumbo mood swings or hadn't noticed.

***

Rita rushed next door, grabbed the baby monitor from LuLu's room, and got her keys and driver's license. "Oh, shoot. Gotta have you." She took her phone off the charger and was ready to slip it under her bra strap when she remembered. "Oops." A quick swipe and tap, and the ringer was off. "Now I'm ready." She saw her tangled cord of earbuds, grunted in frustration, and stuffed them in her pocket. "Now I'm really ready."

Three minutes later, she pulled into the far end of the senior center parking lot. The entrance near the community center dining hall was packed with residents and visitors who made it a part of their weekly routine to enjoy the Saturday morning brunch. Busy with their own day, no one would notice her slipping into the residents' end of the building.

Rita waited for someone to enter through the security door. It wasn't long before an elderly woman on a bright red scooter pulled up. She quickly swiped her key card to open the door, then rolled in. Rita followed her in as nonchalantly as possible. Normally, she'd say hi or mention the weather, but she didn't want to be remembered. Best to be just another visiting granddaughter.

There were two doors to the gym. She tried the first one. Unlocked. She stifled a 'hurray!' and slipped in. Looking around the room, she tried to figure out where the logical place would be for the meeting. A half dozen chairs were already set up. She knew they were for the sitting yoga class, but if she were in charge of a group, she'd make use of what was already there. Directly across from the array was an oversized treadmill. She checked it out, saw it had a cupholder, and decided a little camouflage was needed.

Next to the water fountain was a paper cup dispenser. "Perfect." She punched out the bottom of a cup, wedged the monitor in it so it wasn't poking out the top, then set it in the treadmill's cup holder. "Unless someone's walking or running on this thing, it'll be invisible. Hide in plain sight."

A disturbance outside sent Rita scrambling for the weight room. *Damn! They're early.*

"Oh, lookie there," Eunice said. "Someone already set up the chairs. We have a few minutes before everyone gets here. Let's go see if we can talk our way into a free cup of coffee."

"If you do – and even if you don't – you'd better go tinkle before we start. You know how you are… Tsk, tsk, tsk."

"Knock it off, Euphoria. You're not Mom."

"Yeah, well, someone has to look after you."

The bickering continued as the mismatched twins walked down the hall, leaving the gym empty and Rita a chance to sneak out to the woods. Just as she was leaving the weight room, she heard footfalls.

Familiar footfalls.

Louie! Damn him! Now I'm stuck in here. I'd be fine if those two old biddies hadn't started talking about peeing. Now I have to go.

Rita looked up at the convex mirror and watched Louie. He slipped inside and sidled next to the wall, edging his way down the room so passersby wouldn't see him. When he got to the pile of stacked floor mats, she could practically see a light bulb turn on over his head. He'd found his hiding spot.

Crossing her fingers and her legs, Rita hoped he didn't look up at the wide-angle mirror in the corner and see her. She watched anxiously as he pushed, shoved, and realigned the floor pads of assorted colors, finally establishing his poly-mat fort with a strategically gapped space for a lookout. If she hadn't seen him set it up, she'd never know he was there.

An uncomfortable ten minutes later, Rita squirmed with bladder urgency. She even considered peeing in the discarded Giant Gulp cup someone had tossed in the trash but now it was too late. The league of little old ladies was arriving.

Chatter of recipes for smoked salmon and balms for rheumatism drifted into the baby monitor receiver sitting on the treadmill, their words floating through Bluetooth space to her smartphone, slipping through the white cords of her earbuds. She swatted mindlessly at the tickle on her cheek, the sensation of the thin plastic-coated wire not much different than that of a mosquito landing. *That's it. When the PFD money gets here, I'm buying cordless earbuds. Thank you, State of Alaska for that reverse income tax. May the Permanent Fund Dividend last forever.*

Like a horde of oversized gray lemmings, the women followed each other into the room, plopping through the doorway one by one, like lumps of cold oatmeal into a big bowl. A few moments of milling around, bringing more chairs into the semicircle, and shushing followed until all twelve women were seated. The low hum of confusion was brought to complete silence when the red scooter rolled into the room, the elderly lady

Rita had trailed in holding her smartphone up like a scepter of power.

Rita resisted the urge to sneak another peek at the convex mirror and instead stayed behind the tiny desk in the weight room. She'd have to rely on audio only for the duration.

On the other side of the gym, Louie sat in his tiny spy alcove and closed his eyes, stifling a mega sneeze as a dust bunny from the rearranged mats tickled his nose. Had Rita made it here? Or was she outside, listening through an open window? He squashed the concern, concentrating on rubbing his itchy nose on the shoulder of his tee-shirt, hoping his movement wasn't shifting the mats.

The stillness of the room was eerie. Why was it so quiet if this was a meeting? A woman in the crowd whispered, "When are we…?" and was cut off by a loud air horn. Gratefully, the gasps and groans from the old ladies masked Louie's and Rita's yips of fright coming from the opposite ends of the room.

Ah, there they are. Winifred glanced from the stack of cushioned flooring to the weight room. Two mice had infiltrated her meeting. She looked from her phone to the treadmill. Her 'bug finder' had located it: one of the mice had set up an extra ear to listen in.

The unlikely-looking leader grinned smugly from her motorized ruby throne. "Good morning, ladies. Now that I have your attention, I'd like to thank you for helping our communities with crime control. We may not eradicate it, but maybe we can shoo these criminals into another section of the world. Right now, we'd like to focus on cleaning up midtown."

A hand shot up from the back of the arrangement of chairs. "Yes, Edna – I mean, Eddie."

"If we're working out there, why are we meeting here, twenty-five miles away?"

Winifred grinned broadly and twisted the handle on her scooter, engaging it in a tight circle to park right next to Louie's lookout gap. "To keep the number of moles down."

Taking her clawed grabber stick from its holder on the side of her power cart, Winifred lifted a mat. "Come out and join our group, little mole."

Red-faced and runny-nosed from his stifled sneeze, Louie elbowed his way out of the stinky exercise pads and stumbled upright, wiping his nose on the upper sleeve of his shirt more thoroughly.

"Stop being a child, young man." Winifred reached into the scooter's basket and pulled out a packet of tissues. She tossed it to him. "Now, go pull up a chair and sit in the front row."

The matron of the assemblage backed up her ride, turned around, and sped to the weight room, pausing in front of the open doorway. "Come out, come out, whoever you are," she sang in a sarcastic voice.

Busted.

Rita knew it was no use pretending she wasn't hiding. She eased her way upright, wincing in bladder discomfort. "Can I use the bathroom before I join Louie? I promise I'll be right back. You can even send Minerva with me." Rita waved to the woman she'd met at the donut shop. "Hey, Minerva."

Minerva waved back tentatively, her shock at hearing her name wiped away with a big smile when she recognized Ms. Bismarck, the lady from the bingo game the night before.

For the first time in ages, Winifred was confused. *How did these two know each other? And who was this gawky, snot-nosed man?* She blinked away the shock, glad that only the young red-haired woman had seen her dismay, not her loyal clan. She fluttered her hand in dismissal. "Minerva, go stand outside the restroom and make sure she doesn't get lost coming back."

Louie retrieved a chair and took his time aligning it with the others, then sat and daubed at his dribbling nose, finally giving it an embarrassingly loud, substantial honk. Fidgeting in the hard chair, Louie knew all the old women's bespectacled eyes were focused on him, even without the loud nose blowing. *What's taking Rita so long?*

Seeing her come down the hall – chatting with Minerva like they were catching up on old times – Louie realized Rita would need a chair, too. He popped up and brought one next to his, ignoring the leader's steely glare. What could she do to him? Nothing but make him feel bad about himself. Well, she couldn't do a better job than he was already doing.

"Okay, ladies…" Winifred nodded to Louie, "and gentleman, we are gathered here to discuss very sensitive information. Before we do that, we need to find out why these two are so interested in our group. First, why don't you two introduce yourselves?"

"Ladies first," Louie mumbled, then toned his smirk down to a grin.

Rita glared at him, then shook her head. No use arguing with him. "I'm Rita and I'd rather not give a last name."

"That's quite all right," Winifred said. "We don't use them. Now, why are you here?"

"Because of him," Rita said, canting her head towards Louie. "He thinks he saw something. I just want to verify whether he is or isn't crazy."

"Is he your brother?" Winifred asked.

Both Louie and Rita shook their heads sharply.

"Related in any way?" she pushed.

"He's the father of my child, but we're not romantically involved."

"But were at one time, so there's a history…" Winifred mused softly, so only Louie and Rita heard her.

Rita tipped her chin up and hissed a one-word whisper to the wizened sage, "Tequila."

"Oh… I see. And you, young man?"

"Kind of what she said except my name's Louie."

"And what did you see, Louie, that has you so concerned?"

"I saw my friend, Lily, get shot. Except now that I've met Hana, I think it might have been her. She seems to get around okay. Lily is – or was – older and kind of shuffled around. Hana has a bounce to her step."

"Thank you," Hana said from the back.

"Oh, hey," Louie said, standing up to wave to her.

Small chatter erupted, questions of 'who,' 'how,' and 'when' polluting the formal silence of an inquiry. Winifred held up her smartphone, threatening them with the air horn, and the solemn quietude returned.

"We were down at the port a few days ago. Lily – or Hana – fought off an attacker. Then he – the thug – quick-drawed a gun and shot her. She collapsed and I looked away. When I looked back, everyone was gone."

"You said, 'we.' Who else was there, Louie?"

"Me," Rita said. "I was driving. I didn't see a thing, but there was a big jacked-up Suburban behind me. The big guy in that could have seen it."

"Yeah," Louie added, "and then Rita saw that same ugly rig again, but it had two guys in it this time. But I never saw it. I did see a woman in a gold cape when we got downtown, though."

A burst of tittering from the group was quickly silenced with a glare from Winifred.

"I'm not sure if the caped lady had anything to do with it, though," Louie said. A frown of uncertainty popped up at the chatter behind him, and he added, "But maybe it did."

Winifred took a deep breath to speak but before she could get a word out, Louie stood up. "Ma'am, is my friend Lily still alive?"

"What makes you think I know her?"

"You don't seem to be shocked by any of this. And you don't look like you think I'm crazy. You're interrogating me because you want to know *how much* I know, not *what* I know."

"You're smarter than you look, young man."

"Thanks," Louie said brightly. He paused and scowled, then whispered, "I think."

More snickering from the silver-haired ladies was stilled by Winifred clearing her throat. "So, you're not here to take us out?"

"Why would I do that?" Louie asked. "I just want to make sure Lily's okay. You can wear your flashy capes anywhere you want as far as I'm concerned."

"And I'm just his support crew – more or less," Rita said, shrugging.

"Unless you're hiring," Louie added. "She's unemployed and was supposed to be going to a job interview…"

Rita returned his accusing stare. "I said interview, not 'job' interview."

"Are you sure you aren't siblings?" Winifred asked. "You're acting like it."

"Sorry," Louie mumbled.

"What he said," Rita added softly.

"You two seem harmless enough. Now that you've seen so many of us and appear to know a couple of the ladies in the group, I guess you can stay." Winifred crossed her arms and looked down her nose. "And this is a secret group, so no repeating anything we say in here."

"Oh," Louie said and turned toward Minerva. "So, this is the concerned citizens committee you were talking about. Cool. Hey, ladies!"

Winifred shook her head. Another airhead. "Welcome to the committee, Louie and Rita. I'm Winifred. We're the Spenard Security Society…"

"Sorority," a thin voice called out from the group.

"Symposium," another one countered.

Louie raised his hand, looking around the room then back to Winifred.

"Finally, someone who follows Roberts' Rules of Order. Yes, Louie. You have a question or comment."

"Yes, I do. I don't know about Robert and his rules, but I thought this was the best way to get on a teacher's good side." He paused, uncertain, and walked up to her and whispered, "You are a teacher, or were, right?"

She nodded. "Go ahead."

"If I'm going to be a part of the group, it can't be a sorority 'cause I'm a guy. Just saying…"

Winifred managed to look down her nose as she was looking up at Louie who was towering over her on her scooter. "Well, normally we don't allow men in here, but in your case, we'll make an exception," she said.

"Why? Because I'm gay? I'm just as much a man…"

She cut him off with a wave of her hand. "Gay, straight, whatever: you're still a man. And men are *not* allowed in here.

"However," she motioned for him to come closer, "since you're essentially a non-person with your status with Witness Protection, we'll let it slide. I'm sure you wouldn't want to make an appearance, call attention to your presence, and subvert our whole program."

"How…how did you know about that? It's a big secret," he whispered.

He looked at Rita. She and the others were oblivious to them and their conversation. She was turned around and was chatting with the other ladies, about hair ornaments by their gestures.

"I only told Rita because I had to. She didn't tell you, did she?"

Winifred chuckled. "No, but you just did. I was guessing. By the way, Lily heard that a red-haired young man won the jackpot at bingo. She said maybe it was Lucky, then changed her mind and claimed it was you. She just couldn't believe her young friend was wiped out in a small airplane crash. 'Like a phoenix,' she said, 'Lucky would rise from the ashes and start a new, more vibrant life.'"

"I understood about half of what you said, but I got the gist of it. You're not telling anyone about this, are you? Jess and Arlie would kill me if they found out anyone knew about me in wit-sec."

One side of her mouth turned up, smug with satisfaction, then blossomed into a maternal smile of caring and protection. "No one but I will know. Even if I know that others," she nodded to Rita, "know about your identity status, I'll play ignorant."

"Yeah, sometimes it's good when everyone thinks you're dumb. Believe me, I know."

She motioned him back to her seat. "Okay, now that this meeting is in total disarray…" She steeled herself with a deep breath then let it out. She reached for her phone in the scooter's basket, ready to release the air horn. "Let's see if I can call it back to order."

Louie reached out to stop her. "Can I try a different way to get their attention? I'll be your sergeant-at-arms."

"You can be my page. I already have a sergeant-at-arms." She nodded to a white tee and camo-clad Eddie, standing tall in the back row. Arms crossed, the imposing woman ignored the tittering of the others as she focused on her leader.

"Yeah, she looks tough. I'd hate to bump into her on a heist."

"Well, heists are something we're trying to prevent. More important, though, are the assaults. Robberies are easier to recover from than murders."

Louie's eyes widened. "By the way you were talking, I thought Lily was still alive."

"You thought right. Now, let's get this meeting called to order."

Louie put his fingers in his mouth and blew a loud whistle. "This meeting is now starting," he said in a strong, confident tenor. The noise level decreased but didn't stop entirely. "Hey, listen up or I'm gonna let the boss get your attention."

The talking stopped cold, half the women miming zipping their lips.

"Hey, what's your name?" Louie asked.

"Winifred."

"Winnie Fred?" he asked.

"Speed it up a little, Louie. Winifred."

"Got it." He looked at the group, shoulders back, proud of his new assignment as page – whatever that was – and said, "Presenting Winifred, our leader."

Uncertain applause came from the group. Still standing at Winifred's side, Louie took one step back and brought his hands up, encouraging more clapping. When it reached an appropriate level, he sat down.

"Thank you, Louie," Winifred said, a pink blush coloring her cheeks. "I just wanted to let everyone know that I have taken the footage of our ladies in capes on the job, shot by the different security cameras in the community, and combined them into one video. I put vibrant keywords and hashtags in the description, then released it into cyberspace."

Everyone but Rita and Louie clapped. Their drop-jawed expressions weren't missed by Winifred. "We're running a publicity campaign, showing our prevalence to the Spenard neighborhood first. It won't be too long, and we'll have all of Midtown covered. A few 'set up' robberies and assaults, thwarted by the SSS ladies in capes, and pretty soon, the real bad guys won't want to show their faces."

"Oh…" Rita and Louie said at the same time.

"So, what I saw was Hana getting offed, right?" Louie asked.

"But I didn't really get killed," Hana blurted out. "It still hurt like the dickens, though."

"How'd you do that?" Rita asked. "There was a real bad dude I had seen earlier at Lily's restaurant in the Suburban behind us. He was with the guy who might have been the murderer."

"Operative words, 'might have,'" Winifred said. "I can't tell you anything else other than no one was murdered or seriously injured in that incident."

"But you have witnesses. Or at least one witness: Louie," Rita said.

"And I can't tell anyone about it," Louie said. "For, um, personal reasons."

Winifred tried not to laugh at the man-child's odd combination of boldness and insecurity. "I *will* tell you that we accomplished what we wanted with that very public display."

"Good, because I don't want to get shot again," Hana said loudly.

"No interrupting, please," Louie said. "Raise your hand if you want her attention."

A lady in the back raised her hand.

"Yes, Matilda?" Winifred asked.

"When are the rest of us going to get our capes?"

Minerva put her hand up but didn't wait to be recognized. She blurted out, "And our assignments."

A third woman frantically waved in the air, sucking in her lips so she didn't shout out her comment.

"Yes, Mabel? Do you have a response to the first question?"

"Yes, ma'am. I mean, Winifred. I have the rest of the capes here with me this morning. I brought them in my gym bag. I finally have a purpose for it after all these years. I mean, who needs a gym bag to come down the hall to lift a couple of two-pound dumbbells or walk a mile on the treadmill? I mean, if I got too hot or sweaty, I could go to my own apartment to take a shower. Besides, they don't have a shower here for the gym. I mean, we all live walking distance away." She looked at Louie then Rita. "I mean, most of us do."

Winifred bristled inside with the proliferation of 'I means' but it was just Mabel's nerves acting up. She'd worked long hours on the customized capes for the ladies, even accepting requests for special colors. Her grammar might be atrocious, but her heart was great and pure.

Louie waved his hand in the air and Winifred called on him.

"Hey, do I get a cape, too? I'm not a sister or from Spenard or nothin', but I can be a Señor Security Society crime fighter. But I don't want to go to Anchorage. I can work out here, though, right?"

Rita waved her hand half-heartedly, not expecting to be noticed with all the hubbub and chatter about the new capes. She saw Winifred reach in her cart for her smartphone and quickly plugged both ears.

HONK!

Silence ensued quickly.

"Yes, Rita? You had a question?"

"Yes, Winifred. Since your goal is to reach all over the Municipality of Anchorage, and the median age of your members is in the seventies – maybe sixties with Louie and me bringing down the average – why don't you call it the Senior Security Society…or Symposium or whatever. I don't think there's any way you're going to hide your age, nor should you have to. Bad guys might think twice before robbing a little old lady. She might have some tough protection at hand." Rita mimed karate chops and squirting pepper spray, then grinned.

Winifred fluttered her hands in the air, frustrated at the multitude of questions popping out like mosquitoes at dusk.

"Hey, hush," Louie said. "I mean, order, order!"

When the group had quieted, Winifred said, "Our number one goal is to decrease crime. We can only do that by publicity. We want to do it safely, though. A few high-profile sightings of our caped crusaders squashing crimes, spread by bystanders' videos shot on their phones and uploaded to…" She waved one hand to indicate everywhere. "And we'll get publicity worth millions."

The crowd erupted in applause. Winifred looked over the group, pleased with herself, then saw Rita's doubtful scowl. "Miss Rita, you look uncertain. Would you care to add a comment or offer a suggestion?"

"Believe it or not, I have a little experience here. Naming your group something easy to remember is a good start, but I think you need a little direction when it comes to media streaming."

"Elaborate, please," Winifred said, eyebrows pinched in doubt even as she leaned forward with obvious interest.

"There are venues out there to share posts. We need everyone here to have an active role in reposting. Oh, and it wouldn't be a bad idea for someone to put up posters around town. There aren't enough of you here to cover even the Spenard area, but you can spread propaganda with handbill-sized posters hung on stop signs and power poles, bus shelters, grocery store bulletin boards. Make it a catchy slogan. Something like 'Be good & Beware because SSS have eyes everywhere!'"

"Can you put something like that together?" Winifred asked.

"Me? Why me?"

"Didn't Louie say you were looking for a job, Rita? And you just said you had experience in this."

"Yes, but…but…" Rita huffed in frustration. She started again, a sly smirk arising as she found her out. "Aren't all of you volunteers? I was looking for a paid position."

"Yes, we're all volunteers, but I do have access to funds donated for incidentals. This would be one of them – administration and publicity. Put together a budget and a plan, and I'll look it over."

Rita opened her mouth to protest, then realized she had nothing to say. No excuse. It wasn't human trafficking but helping keep crime off the streets was an honorable goal. Yes, she could help.

"Thank you, ma'am. I'll do it. Just give me your contact info, and we can go from there."

Chapter 13

After Rita and Winifred's private *tête-à-tête* was finished, most of the group erupted into a cacophony of 'ahems' and 'excuse me's' accompanied by handwaving. The most vigorous attention seeker was a broad and boisterous woman with a lilac-colored coif.

Louie stood up and faced the group, then put his fingers to his mouth, ready to whistle. The gesture worked – the group immediately silenced. He smirked in satisfaction and sat down, nodding to Winifred to proceed.

"Yes, Mabel?" she said, rewarding Lady Lilac's efforts.

"These capes are burning a hole in my gym bag. Well, not really, but the ladies have been waiting for weeks for me to get these finished. May I hand them out now?"

Winifred scanned the anxious crowd. They wouldn't pay attention to anything else she said until they had their trophies. "Ladies, make sure you introduce yourselves to our two new members before you leave. And don't crowd Mabel! Form a single file line based on age."

Chairs scooted back and the group shuffled and elbowed their way to Mabel, her gym bag held snug to her body as she headed to the long table at the back of the room.

"Meeting dismissed," Winifred said, certain no one was paying attention.

"Crazy for capes, eh?" Rita asked.

Winifred snorted in disdain. "I thought it was a good idea…"

"It was," Rita said. Seeing the older woman's bitter frustration, she added, "Still is. These women need an identity. 'Concerned Community Committee' meeting once a month in street clothes isn't going to strike fear into anyone. Agents of the Senior Security Society, dashing across town wearing sparkling capes emblazoned with their logo, big superwomen grins of dominance spreading hope to the oppressed… Yeah, you've created a force to be reckoned with. Now the challenge is how to bring it to the attention of the whole population of Anchorage, both the good guys and the bad." Rita nodded, lips pursed in thought. "Yeah, a real challenge."

"Wow. For being so young, you seem to have a tight grip on reality." Winifred shifted positions in her scooter and reached into her pocket for a business card. "Here's my contact information. Don't share it with anyone, even Louie. It's not that I don't trust him, it's just that I feel better knowing *exactly* who knows how to get in touch with me."

"And by that, I assume you have a few false leads out there, scattered around so you know who is trustworthy and who isn't?"

"Sounds to me like you spent a little time underground," Winifred said, her eyes sparkling at meeting a younger version of herself.

"As you said…" Rita said, flipping the card against her thumb before putting it in her back pocket. "Now, is there anything you need me to stay away from? Or is all crime a target?"

"Right now, I'm after the reputation. Whichever group is the most vulnerable to propaganda and the public's passion will work for me."

"Do you have any images or videos I can start with? You did say something about Hana…"

"Shush. Don't mention that out loud," Winifred said. "Ever!"

Rita's head snapped back at the sudden shift in emotional intensity. "Yes, ma'am."

"I'm sorry. That's a *very* sensitive topic. But to answer your first question, yes, I have footage from the scene Louie witnessed at the port, plus the one in Spenard that made the news. If all goes well, by next week, we'll have at least three more. What's your plan?"

Rita looked up and saw Louie chatting with the ladies, several of them gathered around him like he was their favorite grandson who'd just graduated from college. She grinned at the thought, then came back to reality. "Plan? Oh, I think rather than scare the crooks – which might be hard because of the age and gender of our superheroes – I think it would be best to humiliate them. After all, what's worse than being bested by a woman?"

"Being taken down by an *old* woman," Winifred answered. "I like the way you think, Rita."

"If you can't beat 'em with brawn, best them with brains, right?"

Winifred looked at Louie. "Or with luck."

Realizing she'd just given her a clue that she knew Louie's true identity, Winifred switched topics. "Why don't you start introducing yourself and Louie. It might take a while to learn everyone's name. Sometimes I think our parents named us from letters left over from a Scrabble marathon."

Rita chuckled politely, then went to rescue a confused Louie.

"Mabel," the first one said.

"Matilda," the second one said. "And she's Minerva. Got that?"

"Or you can just call all of us Em," Minerva said.

"Call you Em, like you mean you're all Emilys?" Louie asked.

"No," the first woman said, shaking her head in disbelief. "Like the letter M, the first letter of our first names."

The second Em snorted and the third one – Louie already knew her as Minerva, the Nervy –chuckled softly.

Sisterly instincts that Rita didn't even know she had burst to the surface in a growl of derision. "Don't be demeaning Louie. He may not have the same skills as you three. Or any other three people in the world. We all have gifts, blessings, talents; whatever you want to call them. In a bind, I'd rather be standing next to Louie than any other person in the world." She nodded at him and smiled broadly. "Now I know why you had that nickname. You truly are the Luckiest Person in the World, Lucky Louie."

"Yeah, lucky to have you in my life," he said, his hand on her shoulder.

"Sorry about that, Louie," Minerva said. "Everyone's a little tightly wound this morning. Let's start over."

"I know you're Minerva, right?" he asked, glad he had given her the upspoken second name of Nervy to help him remember the first.

The ivory-skinned woman he'd met at the donut shop nodded. "And our super seamstress here is Mabel."

Mabel, Mabel, set the tablecloth. She's the one who made the capes. Like tablecloths draped across their shoulders. "Mabel, glad to meet you," he said and nodded.

"And I'm Matilda," said the silver-haired lady with a flawless coffee-and-cream-colored complexion. "I don't sew, but I can swing a mean handbag if someone tries to mug me."

Silly lady. Tilly. Matilda. Got it! "Nice to meet you, Tilly, I mean, Matilda. Oh, and I guess you already know me. I'm Louie, Winifred's page. That's kind of like an announcer."

"Her herald," Rita said. "And I'm Rita. I guess I'm going to be the rabble-rousing publicity and poster creator."

"Huh?" Louie asked.

"I got a job doing ads for the group, okay?"

"You mean you're gonna get paid and everything?"

Rita shrugged. "Probably enough to buy a coffee now and then. Don't worry. I'll still have plenty of time to be a mommy and editor, in that order."

Louie sighed in relief. "Boy, I sure didn't see this coming when I woke up this morning."

"Yeah, you and me both, Louie. You and me both."

***

"Are you sure she's vetted?" Zero asked.

"Doesn't make a difference," Winifred said on the video chat. "Everything Rita does goes through me. You just keep doing what you need to. I have your back. We'll get the rest of the De Lucas out of Anchorage if it's the last thing we do."

"Well, let's hope it's the next thing, not the last thing."

"Amen to that," Winifred said. "Amen to that."

"Is that you?" Lily asked.

"Depends on which you you're asking about," Winifred sassed, quickly ending her call without a goodbye.

"Yup, it you," Lily replied, shuffling into the light at the bottom of the basement stairs. "Did you bring me something fresh to eat? I tired of tinned and boxed food. Even bag of salad or box of stir-fried rice would be good."

"Not exactly salad but not canned or take-out, either."

Lily slowly climbed up to the landing to discover what fare had been brought in today.

"It's fresh, sort of." Winifred handed her a plastic grocery bag. "Sorry. They didn't have forks. I hope you saved one of those plastic ones from the other day."

"No worries," Lily said. She plucked the two black enameled hair picks from her hair. "I always have chopsticks with me. As long as it not soup, I fine."

She opened the bag. "Ah, fresh veggies with dip and melon bowl. Like Thanksgiving today. Okay. I stay a few days longer. But hurry up. Even if I not really dead, I not want my grandchildren planning my funeral yet. I too young to die."

"You and me both, Lily. You and me both."

Chapter 14

Across town

“I’m telling you, I can handle Zero. He’s here, ready to work, and we need the muscle.”

“We can get muscle anywhere,” De Luca said.

“Yeah, but can we get muscle that isn’t out to take over your job?”

“Grrr.”

“Hey, don’t growl at me, Boss. I don’t want your job, either. I have a girlfriend who likes it that I’m not ambitious. You know what I mean? If I stay well-paid and safe, she’s happy. Well, well-paid and bringing her home trinkets now and then. If I had a high position job like yours, she said the other dames would be all over me, trying to get the goods.” Brutus put his hands between his legs and hefted with a grin. “You know what I mean? That, and they’d want the flash of being the big man’s dame.”

Luca De Luca the Second – the bastard son of one of the former big bosses of the northwest underworld – rolled his eyes. The only purebloods left in Alaska were the benchwarmers. The real A-team had either moved south or were in prison. Not only were the De Luca ‘family’ down to members married to second cousins, most of the first-string players were just referrals – greenhorns, novices – not even road tested. Maybe Brutus was right. He didn’t have a body to prove Zero had taken out that mouthy hostess at Ping’s, but he did have an eyewitness. Plus, the old broad never came back. No one at the restaurant had seen her, either. One way or the other, she was gone.

“Yeah, go ahead and bring Zero in. I may regret it later, but hey, you’re right. As long as he isn’t after my job – and can clean

up a kill that fast and on his own – he has merit."
***

"You're in," Brutus said. "I've set up an introduction for you tonight at dinner. Be at Ping's at four o'clock sharp."

"Isn't that early?" Zero asked.

"You already causin' trouble, askin' questions? And here I vouched for you."

Zero sniffed and swiped at an imaginary mosquito. "Just makin' sure I had the right four o'clock. I didn't think that place was open at four in the morning, but you never know."

"Yeah, well, don't be late and don't be early, either." Brutus started to walk away then turned back. "And take a bath. You smell like you fell in a flower bed."

Zero grunted but didn't reply. Better to say nothing. These people didn't like anyone who thought. The ability – and willingness – to follow through without questions was all they required.

This was gonna be tough.

A trip to the downtown parking garage, a surreptitious entry into a janitor's closet to change clothes, and two flights of stairs climbed to access another vehicle – all without witnesses – and Zero was back to being Zandra.

Why, oh, why did I volunteer for this impossible mission? And why did I use my usual deodorant today instead of that musky crap from the dime store?

Zandra picked up the phone and held down the number eight. A woman's voice drew out the one-word question, "Yeah-uss?"

"I have to come in for a break. Be there in ten."

Zandra ended the call before Winifred could argue the wisdom of being in the same house much less same neighborhood. This was essential. If she didn't take a sanity break, the whole plan would fall apart. Maybe seeing Lily's face – the woman whose life she had saved with this daring ruse – would make a difference.

Hopefully.

Ten minutes later, Zandra was there. She knew the drill. No need to knock. Winifred had the fanciest surveillance equipment in Alaska. Shoot, what she had was more than that. Rumor was she developed it.

The door opened and Winifred was there with her smart-pen, ready to scan Zandra with what looked like an ordinary ballpoint.

'Crap!' Winifred's mouth formed the word, but no sound came out. She swiped her hand across her mouth, miming for Zandra to zip it. Pointing to her with index finger and thumb pinched together, the leader improvised sign language for 'Be Zero.'

Zandra gulped and readied herself to transition again. Shoulders back, she stood up straight, chin out, and climbed into her male gangster persona, despite the floral print dress she was wearing.

"Please, please, put away the gun," Winifred begged. She backed her scooter around and with her claw-tipped grabber, began to noisily knock over vases and picture frames, using her free hand to hastily write a note on the dry-erase shopping list on the table.

'You're kidnapping me,' she scribbled.

Zandra's eyes popped. She had come here for a break, not to compound her stress. An unintentional groan escaped. Rather than stifle it, she multiplied it into a growl. In a flash, he was back in character, snarling as he stomped across the room in sandals, moving like he was a gangster in black leather and boots.

"You're damned right I'm kidnapping you. You've been a pain in the ass since I got to this town. Now, gimme that phone. You're not getting the chance to call for help. Maybe if the boss dangles you in front of the Feds, we might have bait for a swap."

Zandra finished her spiel then threw her hands in the air, her shoulders shrugging, 'What now?'

Winifred waved her smart-pen over her. Zandra knew the routine and pirouetted in place as Winifred performed a closer scan. The light on the pen flashed blue when it crossed over

Zandra's watch. 'Crap!' she mouthed.

Another hand signal: 'Say it out loud.'

Back to being Zero, he angrily shouted, "Crap!"

Winifred popped the lid off her water bottle and held it out to him.

Zero quickly removed his watchband and said, "Get that away from me, you…" before dropping it in, submersing the tattletale listening device in Winifred's cold chamomile tea.

"Did they give you that watch?" Winifred asked, fascinated by the way her friend's face and posture changed between Zero and Zandra so quickly..

"No, it was mine," Zandra sighed. "Brutus asked to see it this morning. He said he wanted to see what kind of step counter it had on it. I told him it didn't have one. He said it did; I probably just didn't know how to activate it. I took it off and showed him. I'll bet that's when he put the mic on it. There's no way it had video capabilities." Zandra shut her eyes, backtracking over the events since she'd been tagged.

Winifred saw the concern and answered it with her phone held up. She tapped a button and replayed their earlier conversation. "I have to come in for a break. Be there in ten."

"That's all you said, my sweet succinct sister in spirit. Any more than that, and we'd be compromised. Now we have to figure out who you were visiting."

"A lover maybe? Coming in for a break could be code for coming in for a quickie." Zandra groaned. "I hope no one cares that I have a lover."

She moved over to the recliner and kicked back, staring at the ceiling, hoping Winifred would say something clever. After a minute of awkward silence, she spoke up. "What's the plan, fearless leader?"

"Well, right now, I've compromised your data stream by throwing water on your watch. You can kidnap me and bring your reputation up a notch."

"Or down," Zandra said. "Remember, Zero's valuable

because he's not ambitious. Zero wouldn't go out and kidnap anyone to impress the boss. That means he's trying to leapfrog over Brutus."

"True. If that's the case, we have to get Brutus involved in this. Damn! I really didn't want to go back in the field. Undercover never was my thing."

"I thought you were a schoolteacher?"

"I was for a few years," Winifred said, holding up the clear bottle to inspect the watch. "Pretty old school. This device is at least five years old. They weren't waterproof back then."

"What? You didn't know that already?" Zandra asked, sitting upright in the chair.

"It was a gamble I had to take. What else could I do?" Winifred chuckled as Zandra sputtered. "Don't worry. I have a plan. Do you have your 'costume' with you?"

She pointed to the gym bag she had dropped at the door when she stepped inside. "Never have it out of my sight. In this game, evidence of crossdressing could get me killed."

"Probably just as quick as if they found you weren't really a gangster."

"Let's hope they never discover either, Winifred. Now, if I'm kidnapping you, where am I supposed to take you? To meet the big boss at a public restaurant? Nah, I don't think so. Either way, I'd feel a lot better if I were wearing the suit. It helps me think like one of them. This," Zandra swished the hem of her pink and red-print skirt with her hand, "stifles my thought process. I'll be right back."

Zandra grabbed the bag and went into the bathroom. Remembering what Brutus said about her flower garden aroma, she turned on the shower. Noticing the only soap was a floral-scented liquid soap, she looked under the sink. "Aha!"

Three minutes later, she was in the living room, red-faced and with wet hair slicked back, chin out with a cocky attitude.

"Whoa! What happened to you?" Winifred asked.

"Nuthin'. Just took a couple minutes to freshen up. Good

thing you had a box of baking soda in there. It may have taken off the first layer of my hide, but it did a fair job of removin' that woman's rose petal stink." Zandra, now coming through as Zero, noticed the wicker bowl of onions and garlic on the counter. He plucked off a clove of garlic, set it on the counter, and thwacked it with the broad side of a butcher knife he took from the block.

"What the…?" Winifred started to protest.

Zero glared at her. "Don't mess with me." He peeled the skin off the garlic and stuck it between his breasts, bound with an elastic bandage. "Smellin' like an Italian kitchen is better than comin' across as a crossdressin' dame. Now, are you gonna do as I say, or do I throw your scrawny hide over my shoulder and haul you out?"

Winifred started to smirk at Zandra, immersing herself in the role-playing, then stopped. If by any stretch of luck or chance Zandra – Zero, she reminded herself – had been followed, she'd best begin her role as victim.

"Please, please, let me keep some dignity. I'll do as you say." Winifred looked around the room, saw her purse, and almost decided against taking it. Would a kidnapper allow a victim to bring one?

"May I take this with me?" she asked meekly. "It has my inhaler and emergency medications in it, and nothing more than a couple of hankies and my wallet."

A sliver of Zandra sneaked into the Zero persona. "Are you sure that's enough?" she whispered.

Winifred nodded with a smug grin. "But I would like to take my water bottle with me. There's a cold one in the fridge."

Zero retrieved it and noting the extra weight of the insulated aluminum container, felt that same smug grin rise on his face. "Come on. We're taking you to meet a business acquaintance of mine."

"You're sure?" Winifred asked, then looked to the dry erase board.

Zero tossed it and the pen to Winifred.

Always able to think quickly even if she couldn't be on her feet, Winifred wrote out a quick note, flashed it to her captor, then quickly erased it and shoved it sideways into the sewing basket of yarn and a half-finished afghan.

This isn't how she'd planned to take down the last of the De Lucas, but it would have to work.

Zero looked over at the decorated wooden plaque halfway up the wall with assorted keys hanging from it. "Looks like your ride's going to have to do, old lady. I don't think I could strap that scooter of yours onto the back of my ride."

This is definitely not how this was supposed to play out! The van conversion wasn't even a month old. Hopefully, there would be nothing more than dings or dents this time around. Bullets through the radiator were harder to explain to the insurance company than a crumpled bumper.

Winifred caught the keys tossed to her and led the way to the garage. The multifunction key fob didn't have marks on it, but she knew what each button was for.

Click!

The garage door opened.

Click!

The engine started.

Click!

The driver's side van door slid open, and a ramp descended. Winifred drove in and pulled up to the steering wheel. A quick push on a button there, and clack-clack – her scooter's wheels were locked in place. She bit off the friendly admonition to 'Come on in. Don't worry. This rig won't bite.'

Instead, she slipped into her victim persona, hoping Zandra was as sharp as her brother had been.

It was ten years ago by the calendar, but the heart didn't use paper to measure time. The loss of Alexander, Zandra's younger brother, was still fresh to both women.

Alexander had been one of Winifred's star pupils. If it hadn't been for the big earthquake he'd still be alive. Instead, the first

Luca De Luca had made use of the police and emergency services distraction to overrun the safe house. Winifred understood Zandra's desire for revenge. It had taken years to come up with a plan, to make sure they could take down the whole empire, not just one man.

Over the last three years, another star pupil and now detective, Arlie Biggar, had taken out most of the De Luca family. What no one had counted on were the bastard sons rising to power. Alonzo's illegitimate son – dark-haired and scrawny Lucky – had no desire to lead the troublemakers. His disappearance had cut the bad guy list down even further. That he had recently reappeared in Chugiak as a blue-eye redhead named Louie was interesting but not a sign of impending trouble.

Hopefully, Luca De Luca the Second was the last one. Whether he died of old age in prison or was tossed down a glacier crevasse by someone he'd crossed, Winifred didn't care. She just wanted 'the family' to disappear.

Zandra, though, had opted to be first strike. She wanted to look into the eyes of her brother's killer before he was gone. By taking on a male assassin's persona, 'Zero' could get close to the boss. When there was enough evidence to send Luca De Luca the Second to prison or – even better, set him up so his own gang would get rid of him – crime would settle down in Anchorage.

Either way, Boss De Luca was destined for hell.

Chapter 15

Lily shuffled from her tidy bedroom alcove across the subterranean basement to the foot of the stairs at the sound of voices. She couldn't help it. Eavesdropping was as natural to her as scratching an itch.

And right now, she felt as if she were covered in mosquito bites. Winifred had a visitor. Or was it two? No one but no one came to see their fearless leader. That's why her home was the perfect hideout, the safest of safe houses.

Even so, Winifred had given Lily one unbreakable rule: do not come upstairs. Lily wasn't locked in. She did have to climb to the top of the stairs to retrieve her food, but she never went beyond the threshold, never into the kitchen or even the hall. The two women operated on the trust system. Trust that if Lily didn't obey Winifred's rules, they'd both be goners.

'The next – and only – time you are to come out of this basement is for our victory celebration. It's only a matter of days before these men will have turned against each other. Finally, the streets will be clear.'

Winifred had assured her it wouldn't take too long for their game of deceptions to be over. The staged murder of 'Lily' by a new player in town – Zero – was a great distraction so the book of accounts could be extracted. After falsifying the data and reinserting the ledger into its hidden cubby, conflict within the organization would arise. Luca De Luca the Second's rage and shortsightedness would flare. Animosity between De Luca and his subcontractors would crank up to extermination level, and the rival gangs would wipe each other out.

At least, that was Winifred's theory.

Lily didn't believe it. In her sixty years, she had lived through multiple generations of gangs and family rivalries in three countries, on two different continents. One thing always stayed the same: when you stomped out one cockroach, another was there to take its place. There would always be criminals.

Rumble, rumble, rumble.

The garage door was opening.

Rumble, rumble, rumble.

And now it was closing. Winifred never left without saying goodbye.

Lily went to the laptop she used. No messages or emails about her departure, either.

Clatter. Click. Stomp, stomp.

Okay, now someone had come back into the house. That movement wasn't Winifred. She didn't walk much less stomp like she was knocking snow off her boots. Besides, it was summer.

"Can't forget you, my little time bomb," a deep voice said.

Lily stood at the bottom of the stairs, listening.

Screech. Thunk.

Damn! Someone had opened the roll-top desk. By the delay between the unique sound of the warped wood opening and the thud of it shutting, it sounded as if someone got the doctored ledger.

Double damn! Winifred's been kidnapped and the fake set of books stolen.

Slam!

Lily waited to make sure the culprit was gone. Not even two seconds later, she heard the door open again. The doorknob jiggled as someone had locked it from inside, then the warped door was slammed shut again.

She had to get help, but from who? Lily thought of the many ladies in their group, but she couldn't remember their names. Most of the names started with the letter M. They told her to just call them Em. That worked fine when they were face-to-face but didn't help now. Wait! The two who insisted they were identical twins. They were Europa and… Dang! What difference did it make? She didn't have their phone numbers or email addresses.

Aha! But they *were* all members of ALL: Alaska Lovers of LOST. The fan club had monthly brunch meetings in town. That was how they'd all met. She'd reach out on their fan site, post a cryptic message, and grab the attention of one of her ladies.

Then, after she verified the respondent was really a member of the SSS Caped Crusaders – or whatever they were calling themselves this week – she'd open a private chat window and ask for help. Certainly, someone would come to rescue her. After all, how could she find Winifred without a car?

Lily opened the fan page, scanned the latest comments, then realized she was getting distracted with the posts. She grabbed the keyboard and started a new thread of conversation.

"'I think Jody Pomeroy is a Stuborn-Stuped-Scott!' There! That ought to get some attention. Whether they agree or not, I know at least one of my ladies will want to correct my spelling."

The comments and frowny faces were popping up almost faster than she could read them. "There! The Purple Queen! That's the tall twin's username. Yup. She couldn't resist fixing my spelling."

Lily typed in 'SSS is shorthand for him, no matter how you spell."

Bink!

A chat window popped up on Lily's screen. 'Who R U?'

'Name sounds silly' she typed in.

No response.

Lily added, 'Trouble. Can U help?'

'Not Willy or Nilly then?' came up.

'Not Billy or Dilly neither.'

'Either,' Euphoria typed. 'I'll be there ASAP.'

'Fast is better.' Lily pushed the keyboard away and sat back. "I guess I break my promise and go upstairs, Winifred," she said to the monitor. "What else to do?"

Euphoria shut the laptop and stood up. "Hey, sis. We have an emergency. Grab your cape. We might need it."

"Huh?" Eunice asked. "But I just mixed up a batch of

chocolate chip cookies."

"Put a plate on the bowl and stick it in the fridge. We have an SOS for the SSS via the LOST fan site."

"Who? What?" Eunice asked, her mouth full of a big bite of purloined cookie dough.

"Lily sent me a coded message. I think Winifred's in trouble."

***

Five minutes later, the sisters pulled up to Winifred's house in their gold-tone minivan. "Do I put my cape on now or later?" Eunice asked.

"Not now and I don't know about later because I don't know what's going on. Let's just go in casual, like we're popping over for tea or something."

"Euphoria, no one pops over for tea anymore."

"Okay, so we're popping over for a LOST marathon," Euphoria said, "since the fan site's where I got the encrypted message."

"Now, that's more like it." Eunice rang the doorbell, waited to the count of three, then rapped on the brass door knocker and rang the bell again.

"Stop that," Euphoria said. "You're acting all antsy and drawing attention. Here, let's just go in." She turned the knob. "It's locked. I'll use my credit card to break in."

The door opened quickly, but only a few inches. "Is it you, sisters?"

"It's us, Eunice and Euphoria," Eunice said brightly.

"Not so loud…" Euphoria scolded.

Lily pulled the door open a few inches further. "Quick. Come in."

The two sisters tried to enter at the same time, shouldering one another out of the way, neither one wanting to give in to the other.

When she saw the problem was their contention, Lily stepped back and opened the door all the way. Both women tumbled forward and nearly fell over the back of the couch. Bickering started immediately but was quelled by Lily's sharp whistle.

"Stop being babies," Lily scolded. "This serious. Winifred gone and she not say goodbye."

"Oh, good grief," Eunice huffed. "Since when did she need to give you a farewell? We all know she's just one lame excuse short of being rude."

"It not that. There were voices and stomping. I heard her car leave, too." Lily shuffled over to the roll-top desk. She tried hefting the cover, but it was stuck. Euphoria came over and lifted it with ease.

"Thank you," Lily said with a quick nod. "See! Ledger with doctored numbers. It gone! Someone take Winifred and the book!"

"How do you know it wasn't just her grabbing it for her switcheroo and forgetting to say goodbye?"

"Europa, Winifred on electric scooter. If she not walk, how she stomp?"

"The name's Euphoria," she said. "And good point."

"Maybe you should put number four on your forehead, so people remember," Lily said, then chuckled at her joke.

"Before we go *stomping* off on our own," Eunice said, "tell us everything that happened up to when you locked the door and reached out to us."

"I no lock door. I heard furniture crashing," she pointed out books and knickknacks scattered around the room, "one or two people plus Winifred, stomping, garage door open and shut, and front door open and shut."

"Why would they come in the front door if they drove out the garage?" Euphoria asked.

Lily let out a huff of exasperation. "He come back to get ledger." Her eyes widened. "But when he leave, he lock door again. What kidnapper leave mess, take woman and book, but lock door so no one come in?"

Both sisters shrugged and looked at each other. "I don't know," Eunice said.

"I give up," Euphoria added.

Lily brought up her hand and giggled behind it. "Kidnapper who part of SSS, that who!"

Stunned, the sisters took a moment to stare at each other. Finally, Euphoria spoke up. "How do you figure that?"

"Kidnapper want to make sure no one come in and bother me."

"She has a point," Eunice said. "But we only have women in the group."

"Except for Louie. Do you think it's him?" Euphoria asked.

Lily shook her head vigorously, her eyes cast down so her smirk didn't betray her. Once she had it under control, she looked up. "Not everyone is as she seems. That all I say."

"So, let's go find our fearless leader," Eunice crowed, arm raised in victory, ready to lead the charge.

"No, no, no," Lily said. "First we wait. She get word to us, I sure. We need to call emergency meeting and let everyone know what happen." She looked at the clock on the mantle. "I think it good time for yoga class, yes?"

"Huh?" Eunice asked.

Euphoria nudged her and scowled. "Yes, I do. Grab whatever you need, plus put on a hat or something. We don't want to chance anyone seeing you."

Lily shuffled to the bathroom and came out wearing a yellow scarf and big dark-rimmed sunglasses. "Look good to you?" she asked.

Euphoria glanced at her feet. The black sandals with split-toed white socks were a sure giveaway. "Eunice, swap shoes with her."

Obeying without question, the smaller sister nudged off her slip-on canvas shoes. "Now what am I going to wear?"

Lily stepped out of her sandals and into the alternative footwear. "Ooh! These nice. Maybe too big, but nice."

Euphoria kicked the sandals over to Eunice. "Just pretend we're playing dress up. You can be the Japanese Barbie doll."

Eunice looked at Lily and imitated her remark. "Ooh, these nice! At least, for now. I don't think they'd work this winter."

"Not too good in summer rain, either. For inside, they fine. Now, we go to yoga class." Lily chuckled. "Or what we call yoga class. We get twisted up in other way in 'not emergency' meeting."

***

"Hey, Rita," Jess said, knocking on the door as he entered.

"Boundaries, dude," she said, shutting her laptop. "You just missed nude yoga by about ten minutes."

"Ew. Okay. In the meantime, I wouldn't be offended if you put a chain up. It might help me remember."

"Nope. Tina has weird hours. I don't want to lock her out. So, what can I help you with?"

"Is Louie acting a little weird to you?"

"You mean weirder?" Her chuckle ended in a quick snort. "Sorry, that was rude. Sort of."

"Not that. To me, that's part of his charm. What I'm talking about is he seems a little paranoid. Flipping on the light switch first and double-checking the room before he enters, standing sideways when he opens the mailbox like he's expecting it to explode…"

Rita blushed, knowing the reason – their involvement with the Senior Security Society – but certain she'd better keep the *whole answer* to his question to herself. "You know when this started, right? When he told me about his involvement with Witness Protection. Part of him is afraid of his old family and the guys he used to run with."

"But they're all in prisons down south somewhere," Jess said, his hands up in exasperation. "I even read him a list of who was where and for how long, hoping he'd chill out."

"Well, he's also a dad now. He's watching out for our little girl."

Jess blew out some of his exasperation. "We *all* have that same protector attitude running herd over everything we do. That's not it."

"Okay. Here it is, Jess. He's afraid of Arlie."

"Oh, hell no. He and Arlie are tight. He considers him his brother-in-law, even though he and Charlene aren't siblings."

"All the more reason for him to be afraid. He sees it as only trust that holds them all together. Now that he's betrayed Arlie by telling us he's in Witness Protection, he's afraid… Hell, I don't know what he's afraid of. Maybe he's afraid Arlie will ship him somewhere and break up our perfectly imperfect little family."

Jess chuckled. "He'd have to go through me and the whole federal government to do that. And last time I looked, federal agencies trumped the Anchorage Police Department."

"Don't get cocky, Mister FBI," Rita said. "He's just overly protective and slightly insecure."

"Insecure about what?"

"Not having a job. Shoot! Look at me. I was in the same boat until yesterday. Now I'm in seventh heaven with a part time job making memes and posters for a group of little old lady volunteers. Geez! How desperate can a woman get?"

"But he's writing a book. Doesn't that count for something?" Jess looked around, suddenly feeling ill at ease.

"Uh, oh," Rita said. "Did that sixth sense of yours just kick in?"

He grimaced and paused. "Shit! I left the bacon on!" he said and darted out the door without shutting it.

"Bacon and pancakes for breakfast. Well-done on the bacon. Works for me, even if I have to wash dishes afterward," Rita said and closed out the programs on her laptop.

"There you are," Louie said when Jess dashed in the room. "They might be a little on the crispy side, but I like bacon that way. Hey, what do you think about going to the zoo two days in a row? I'm going to give up on writing. I guess I'm just not cut out for it."

“You’re not a quitter, Louie.”

“Yes, I am. I quit my life as a… you know. My former life is no more. I quit it. Zap. Wiped out. Nada.”

“You transitioned. You were a creepy crawly caterpillar, sly enough to keep away from the crows that were picking Anchorage clean, crapping on people wherever they flew. So what if you don’t know what your final occupation is going to be? It’s called a chrysalis stage – you know, you’re inside a cocoon, changing into a butterfly. Besides, how long have you been writing that book?”

“You mean, trying to write that book. Shoot, Jess,” Louie forked the bacon onto a plate covered with paper towels, “I don’t even have a title.”

“Just write. It doesn’t have to be about anything in particular. I took an art class once. I insisted I couldn’t draw. The teacher said, ‘Draw a dot.’ I did. ‘Draw a circle around it. Add a few squiggly lines…’ Next thing you know, I had an awesome paisley design. It all started with a dot. Just write a word. Add another. Look out the window and describe what you see. I’ll bet the first thing you see is different from what I notice. It might take a while, but I’ll bet you find a theme.”

Beep-beep!

Louie took out his phone and looked at the text. ‘Yoga class at ten. Be there.’ He frowned, then went wide-eyed.

“What’s that?” Jess asked.

“I think I’ll start by writing a short story about a bunch of randy little old ladies taking up yoga to keep in shape.”

“Huh?”

“Oh, I’ve been hanging out at the senior center. I met a few of the old folks on the shuttle bus. We’ve played bingo, that sort of thing. I was just invited to a yoga class at ten. Who knows, maybe I’ll take a few pictures and write a bestseller on Yoga to Reverse Aging.”

Jess put his arm around Louie’s shoulder and kissed him on the cheek, making sure he didn’t distract him too much.

"Whatever makes you happy, dear, is fine with me. I've got LuLu under control." He nodded to the little girl seated in the middle of the room, bouncing her stuffed rabbit on her lap, singing it a nonsense song. "Just keep out of Anchorage, okay?"

Louie blinked quickly, then looked at Jess. "Sure, no problem."

***

Knock, knock.

"Come in, Louie," Rita said. "The door's unlocked."

"What did you say to Jess?" Louie asked, trying to make sure he didn't sound as angry as he felt at the betrayal.

"Nothing, really. Just talked about you and writing and my new job. Babble and B.S., pretty much. Why?"

"He just told me to keep out of Anchorage."

"Really? Hey, I promise, it had nothing to do with anything we said."

"Do you think he knows something we don't?"

"I'm certain Jess knows a *lot* we don't, Louie. It's a huge part of what he does: information."

"I mean about," he leaned in and whispered, "the De Lucas."

"I think Jess was right."

Louie's back straightened, both indignant and defensive. "Right about what?"

"You're acting weird."

Beep-beep.

Louie looked down at his phone, then up at Rita. "It says to bring Rita – we don't have her number."

"Bring Rita what?"

"I think the SSS ladies are having a meeting. They're calling it a yoga class. It starts at ten. Do you think you can give me a ride?"

"And our daughter?"

"Jess said to go, he had it all under control."

"Well, before we scoot, I'm grabbing some bacon. I guess it's a good thing he isn't a pastry chef, or I'd be as big as the couch." She shut her laptop for the third time in twenty minutes. "I'm glad we'll be seeing Winifred. I emailed her some mockups of posters but I don't know if she got them. I'll show them to her on my phone."

After giving LuLu a few hugs and kisses, the two were on their way. Rita clicked on the CD player. 'Staying Alive' by the Bee Gees blared out.

"Why do you always play that when we're going out?" Louie asked.

"Only to the senior center. It's an OCD thing, I think. It takes as long to get there in the summer as that song is long. I haven't found the right song for winter."

"And you said I was weird."

***

The group was milling about, some leaning on the backs of the chairs, others seated. "Where's our fearless leader?" Louie asked. "I want to announce her."

"It's ten o'clock on the nose and she's not here," Eddie said. "I think something's wrong. She's never late."

"Sorry about that," Euphoria said as she burst through the door, Eunice and a bent-over woman in a yellow head scarp shuffling in behind her. "I hate being late. I knew when my Flashdance album started playing over again we were running behind."

Rita chuckled and everyone else looked confused.

Eunice popped in, "From our friend's place in Anchorage to here is exactly the length of the Flashdance soundtrack. She started it before we were all buckled in, though. I told you to wait until Lil…"

Euphoria reached over and clamped a long-fingered hand over her sister's mouth.

"Lily!" Louie squealed, rushing over to pick her up and spin her around in a huge bear hug. He kissed her on both cheeks before gently setting her down. "You don't know how glad I am to know you're alive. I thought I saw someone shoot you."

“Hey,” Hana called out, waving frantically to Lily.

“Hana!” Lily replied and shuffled toward her niece, the two meeting in a full embrace. “You saved my life. Thank you, thank you, thank you.”

“Well,” Hana said with a chagrined smile, “you’d do the same for me if you could. But…but why are you here? Aren’t you supposed to be in hiding?”

Lily finished removing the scarf that had come off during all the hugging and put it back on, pushing the glasses up her nose to reassume her incognito appearance. “This is best I could do for now. We have to have meeting.” She looked around the room, recognizing a couple of faces, the others new to her. “Winifred is kidnapped,” she said in a soft voice.

“Wait! What?” Eddie asked, stepping forward to begin an interrogation.

Euphoria stepped in between them. “Let’s all sit down and remember Robert’s Rules of Order.”

“Who put you in charge?” Eunice asked, her head tilted back, and bottom lip stuck out.

“Me,” Euphoria answered, her huge brown hands balled into fists, knuckles placed on her broad hips. “Eddie, would you secure the doors? Everyone else, park it, so we can figure out how to rescue our Winifred.”

Chapter 16

"Who knows where Winifred lives?" Euphoria asked the group.

Everyone but Louie and Rita raised their hands.

"I told her that was reckless," Eddie mumbled. Euphoria glared at the remark but the former marine shrugged, unintimidated by the six-foot-plus Pacific Islander who had assumed command of the group. Size meant nothing to her.

"Okay, next question," Euphoria said. "Does anyone have any idea where the kidnapper would take Winifred? Is she safe? Did she take her emergency meds with her?"

Lily waved and stood up, shuffling to the side of Euphoria. She turned and addressed the group. "Winifred not really kidnapped," she whispered.

'What's and huh's?' peppered the airspace as everyone leaned forward or turned up volume controls on hearing aids to hear better.

"Did you say she wasn't kidnapped?" Eddie asked, kneeling beside the older woman as if afraid she'd fall apart and wanted to be near to pick up the pieces.

"Don't tell 'em," Hana – Lily's body double – shouted from the back of the group.

"Don't tell us what?" Euphoria growled.

"Everyone sit down and listen," Lily ordered, her 'Grandma Zumu is in charge' persona taking over.

They all – including the belligerent Eddie and Euphoria – did as ordered.

"Yes, our leader is kidnapped. She is safe. Kidnapper is someone I know. And Winifred know, too. I also know where she is. Sort of."

Lily paused and looked to Louie, then Rita. "This father of your baby girl?"

Rita nodded.

Louie opened his mouth to say more, but Rita – anticipating it – already had her elbow at the ready and nudged him to stifle it.

"What do you mean you know where she is being held, sort of?" Rita asked.

"I write coordinates on fortune cookies I gave you when you come to restaurant. Lucky numbers for Lucky."

"I'm not Lucky," Louie said, scowling at her not to reveal his former name.

"Yes, you are," Minerva said. "You won the bingo jackpot last night."

"Oh, yeah. I guess I am. Lucky Louie," he said and chuckled nervously, realizing she could have meant he was fortunate, not the man named Lucky. He turned to Rita. "Did you save your numbers?"

She reached in her front pocket and took out her packet of cash folded over her driver's license and debit card. "Yeah, I did. Since Jess and Tina came back before we could have them play the lottery, I figured I'd save the numbers for the next time they went south."

"Oh, yeah. That's what I did, too." He reached in his back pocket and took out his wallet. "Great minds think alike, I guess."

"And then there's Lily," Rita said. "Great plan, Lily. Oh, and I'm glad to see you're alive."

"Me, too. Who best map reader here?" Lily asked, looking deep into the faces of the women. Even though no one answered in the affirmative, she saw the smug look of confidence on Eddie's face. The too-young-to-be-a-senior woman in a casual white tee and camo cargo pants had a self-assurance not attached to pride or cockiness. A soldier.

Lily pointed to Eddie. "You military?"

"Yes, I was. And I can read a map well enough."

"You two," Lily said, indicating Rita and Louie. "Give her your numbers."

"Hold on a sec." Rita took Louie's fortune cookie insert and her own, set them on the seat of the folding chair, and snapped a quick photo with her phone. "Okay. Here you go. I just wanted to make sure we had a backup."

Eddie took the slips of paper and did the same thing. "Now we have two. Besides, this is easier to read at night." She looked out the window – the twenty hours of summertime daylight that never went totally dark – and amended her remark. "Easier to read if I'm in a dark spot."

"We need a plan, ladies," Euphoria said.

"Excuse me," Lily said, her hand waving furiously, dismissing her. She looked up and addressed the woman who was twice her size. "Did Winifred tell you what to do?"

"Well, no." Euphoria realized the little old woman had put her on the defensive. She stood tall and smirked as she looked to the group. "Did she tell you?"

"Yes, she did." Lily ignored the power play challenge and took over as the person in charge. "You, Rita?"

Rita nodded.

"She ask you to make posters, right?"

"Yes. I have the preliminaries here. I emailed them to her this morning, but I never heard back."

"That because she not get chance. I saw them, too. She like one with De Luca looking like pig, rolling in mud you name as crime."

Rita chuckled. "Yeah, I figured it was easier to label it than try to create a cartoon representation of the filth of drugs and extortion."

Lily waved the comment away. "You go to printer and make many copies. Give each woman here this many," she indicated a two-inch width, "to put up all over Anchorage."

Minerva raised her hand and started speaking at the same time. A collective groan at the procedural error was stifled by her remark. "If Rita emails thc file to all of us, we can make our own copies. Winifred already assigned us our territories, or rather, zones. She said when the time came, we could put on our capes and spread the word. Oh, and we could even enlist younger folks, like teenage grandkids, to help us. I don't know how much the printing is going to cost, but I'll cover the cost of the ones I get. That slimeball De Luca was responsible for my niece's husband's death. I want him gone!"

"Here! Here!" and "You tell 'ems," rang through the room.

"Okay, here you go, ladies," Rita said, tapping on her phone screen.

Ding! Ding! and other assorted email notifications chirped all at once.

"But…but…" Louie protested, then his phone *beep-beeped.*

"Hey, Winifred gave me everyone's email addresses, including yours," Rita said. "And before you ask, no, I didn't give it to her. From what I understand, she's a very clever woman."

"Yeah," Eddie said. "She'd never brag, but she's as sharp as they come. I'm not too surprised Winifred already had a rescue plan in place before she knew she'd be kidnapped."

"But how is putting up posters going to help?" Louie asked.

"Pig pictures bother De Luca very much," Lily said. "He will send all his men to take them down. That leave his secret hiding place unguarded. Then Winifred can do what she needs to do."

"Hey, I can help. I used to hang out there. I know that place better than anyone here, for sure."

"No," Lily said firmly. "You father now. You stay and take care of your daughter with not-your-wife-or-girlfriend."

Rita chuckled at her new designation. "Oh, and your fiancé doesn't want you going into town anyhow. Just hang out here. I'm sure there's something for you to do."

Ahem.

Everyone looked to Eddie, her hand up halfway, her gray eyes steely as she sought their attention.

"Was there another one of these?" she asked, holding up the two slips of paper.

"Oh, yeah," Louie said. "This one was for our daughter. Her

name is LuLu. She's named after me."

"They know that already, Louie. I'm sure you've told that to everyone you've ever met." Rita groaned in exasperation. "No doubt, you'll keep telling them, too."

Eddie looked at the cryptic message. "Hmm. This script is different. Lily, did you write this one or did Winifred?"

"What? Oh, let me see."

Eddie showed her the paper Louie had just given her.

Lily said, "Oops. Winifred give me that. It goes with this." She pulled a two-by-three-inch silk envelope out of her waistband. "These instructions for you in case something happen to her."

"What time did she get kidnapped?"

Lily beamed at Eddie with certainty. "9:10. I look at clock when I hear voices upstairs. I remember because numbers come one after other, like counting."

"Okay, ladies." Eddie looked at Louie, "and gentleman. We have just over twenty-two hours to plaster Anchorage with these posters. Don't bother with the outlying areas. If your zone is out here in the Eagle River area or south towards Potters Marsh, we need you to come help cover the downtown and mid-town zones."

"Is that what those numbers said to do?" Louie asked. "Because the one I gave you didn't look like a message to me."

Eddie chuckled. "You weren't in Special Ops, were you?"

"Huh?"

Rita nudged him, then looked up to the new field commander. "Please excuse him. He wasn't in the service, but he does have inside intel. Just think of him as your mole who's located to the outside. He's probably the most valuable person in the room that way."

Eddie's smugness evaporated. "I can respect that. Come on, let's talk. Everyone else, get to making and distributing those handbills. I want every power pole and bus shelter downtown covered. Cafés, pawnshops, anywhere you think these guys might hang out or harass folks. If anyone asks what you're doing, tell them you're working to stomp out crime and secure the future for your family."

Rita bent to her phone and started typing. "Those are great words for the next posters."

"Yeah, well, if we do this right, we won't need any more," Louie said.

Lily listened and shook her head. "If only it that easy. If only."

***

Late that afternoon, Brutus came into Ping's Restaurant. "Is he here?" he asked the young hostess.

"Sorry," Jennifer said. "Who you looking for?"

"The boss. You know, the big guy I hang out with when I'm here."

"Oh, potsticker man," she said with a forced congenial smile. "He in back with other man."

Jennifer led the way, holding the menus close to her chest. They weren't a shield, but the layers of laminated paper felt like one. Whenever near these men in black, she felt vulnerable. Had Zumu felt the same way? Probably not. Her boldness might have been why she disappeared.

"Hey, Boss," Brutus said, interrupting the conversation between him and Zero. "I hate to barge in like this, but we have a problem." He thrust out a fistful of posters, their corners ragged from being torn down.

Luca De Luca the Second set them down on the table then looked around as he pulled out his reading glasses. "Can's see a damn thing in this dim light without them," he muttered.

Eyes wide, he read the top paper, then shuffled through the others, looking to see if they were all the same. "Where'd you get these?" he grumbled.

Zero leaned forward and glanced at the paper. *Whoever had made this was gifted. The caricature of De Luca as a fat pig was spot on. Even without his name tagged on his coat, he was identifiable.* A little smile of pride started to tickle his upper lip, but he stifled it, picking up the cup of hot tea to cover it. He couldn't let Zandra out. This was Zero's time to shine.

"These are all over town," Brutus said. "I started tearing down every one I saw, then…then. Then I had to stop. There were too many. I came back here to tell you."

"Call the gang. Get every man on cleanup detail."

"But what about whoever's putting them up?" Brutus asked.

"We can't do anything in broad daylight. We'll have to ID him, then put a tail on him. A little thunk-thunk in a dark alley and we'll be done." De Luca looked at Zero and grinned. "Sound like something you're up for? Break your teeth and show your worth to your new boss?"

A little whisper of an angel fluttered above Zero's head, giving him comfort in the fact the crack in character was mended and he was back, rock solid in the Zero persona. "Piece of cake," he grunted.

"Hey, Boss," Brutus said, "you think maybe I can get the rest of the day off? It's my anniversary and my lady is bugging me…"

De Luca glared at him, then realized that Brutus was loyal but wouldn't be worth a dime if he was pining and whining about that old lady of his. "Yeah, yeah. Whatever. Make sure you have the guys lined out on cleaning up this trash. I don't want one block missed. After you're done with that, scram. Zero's gonna clean up the loose ends, right?"

Zero snorted with a hit man's assurance. "I got this. Let me make a few calls and see if I can 'zero' in on the latest activity. Meter maids and cops ain't too keen on civilians pasting up flyers on public property. I might find out a little from some of my birdies."

De Luca chuckled. "I was wondering how you got that name. Sure, whatever. Just remember, if you ever try to cross me or any of my A team, you'll be a zero of another kind."

Unintimidated by the crime leader who was just hours away

from losing his throne in the hierarchy of archcriminals, Zero laughed out loud. "Yeah, zero trace of me or my DNA. Right, Boss?"

"Right…"

"Then I'll get *right* on it." Zero looked up and saw the young hostess come to their table with a steaming bowl of potstickers and a bowl of brown sauce. "I'll pass on dinner, but thanks anyhow, little lady." He pulled a twenty-dollar bill out of his vest pocket and stuffed it in the front pocket of her apron. "Don't spend it all in one place."

Jennifer nodded, shocked at the familiarity of the man she'd only seen once. Still, something seemed familiar. She set the tray with the food in front of De Luca and Brutus. "For you. Very hot. Don't burn yourself."

"Yeah, yeah, yeah," De Luca said, shooing her away with a flick of his wrist. "I'll be the judge of that."

Jennifer went into the kitchen and sat down by the back door. Propped open to let out the excess heat, it created its own aura of peace. She took out the tip and unfolded the bill. "Get out!" was written on it. She looked up and saw the man who had given it to her climb onto a motorcycle. He waddled backwards, reversing his big Harley step by step. The heavy helmet covered his face, but the clothes were recognizable as the heavy tipper.

Once out of the parking spot, the rider turned to her and gave her a thumbs up, the visor up. He smiled broadly, showing teeth and sincere glee. Her high school civics teacher! Miss Zandra was the new thug in town!

"Hey, Joe," she said to her cousin, the cook. "I don't feel too good. I think I'd better take off."

"Yeah, you and me both," he said, untying his apron. "Must be something going around."

"Wait. What? We both can't leave."

"Why not? Don't worry. I'll stay long enough to let those bad boys know that when they're done, I'm shutting down the joint." Joe started scratching the back of his neck. "Whatever it is, it's driving me nuts."

"So, you don't have the flu? Is it something contagious?"

"Hell, if I know. My gut's fine." He started squirming and scratching everywhere. "Damn! I want to crawl out of my skin!"

"Please, don't do that. Come here. Let me see what's going on in the daylight."

Joe came over and stood in the bright afternoon sun. "What do you think it is? Is it some kind of rash? Do you think I can I get rid of it with a cream or something?"

Jennifer pushed his neck forward, inspected the base of his head, and chuckled. "Well, in my opinion you have one or both of two possible problems…"

He pulled away at her laugh. "Well, what are they?"

"It looks like head lice, but also skin irritation. What kind of laundry detergent are you using?"

"Detergent? You mean for washing my clothes? Nothing special. I just scoop out a big baggie of the stuff we use for the dishes here."

"That's for heavy grease. It's probably stripped off all your natural body oils and you're flaking away. But I'm pretty sure you have lice, too. Get some of that super gentle liquid soap they use for washing babies for the rash. But before you take a shower, shave your head. Oh, and any other body parts that have hair. Lice don't care where they make their little nests as long as they can lay their little eggs on hair."

"Ew! So much for swiping Leon's knit hat. I'll bet that's where I got the lice."

"Instant karma. You go tell the bad boys in black we have an emergency, and I'll put up the closed sign. I don't know why business has been so bad lately, but I don't doubt the De Luca's have something to do with it."

"Yeah, that and the disappearance of a few family members. Now Ping's gone, too."

***

"I feel so useless," Louie moaned. "Jess and Tina took LuLu

for a revisit to the zoo, so no kid to watch, I'm uninspired to write, you get to go wherever you want to put up posters and fight crime…"

"Hey, Louie. I have news for you. Jess and LuLu aren't responsible for your happiness, and neither am I. It's all up to you. Eddie has your contact info. I'm sure she'll call you if she needs help. Oh, and if you're looking to feel fulfilled or useful, there's lots of ground in the backyard you can clear for our vegetable garden. As soon as it's weeded, tilled, and hilled, we can put in peas."

"How's that going to make me happy?"

"Um, don't you want to have LuLu help you poke peas in the soil? Can't you see yourself coming out here with her, watching them grow day by day, showing her how the flower turns into a pea pod…"

"Oh, yeah. I think I read about that in school somewhere."

"Well, then both of you can learn at the same time. Oh, and plug in your phone. Jess just texted me and asked me to tell you he couldn't get through to ask you to switch over the laundry."

She fished the neon-colored rainbow keyring out of her back pocket and flashed it at him. "I'm going to take off. Tina left me her tin can of a car. It isn't much, but it'll get me downtown. I don't trust those little old ladies to get it done without supervision."

"Why not?" Louie scratched his head. "They're smart enough to have stayed alive all these years. They've done a lot of things right."

"True," Rita said, her cheeks reddening at showing prejudice towards older people. "And rather than whimper about what *you can't* do, do something constructive! Or at least stay busy and pretend to be happy. You weren't put on this earth to sit around and whine."

"Okay, *genius*," he said with a scowl, "then why am I here?"

"Maybe it's to make this a better place for others, for those who can't do for themselves or…or just to clean up the planet and make it a healthier, safer air, dirt, and water environment." She paused and added, "Now I know what you mean about making the word genius sound like a slur. I really am sorry about that."

"Yeah, I'm sorry, too. Get going. I have this. Maybe I can alphabetize the canned goods or something."

"Write your book, Louie. Remember what both Jess and I said, 'Just write!' Shoot, write about alphabetizing those canned goods or a hundred and one things to do when you're bored."

"Now, that's a good topic!" He looked around the room. "Where do I start…"

Rita left him to his musings, glad she'd been a help. Now hopefully whatever Eddie had found in that cryptic fortune told her what to do next because she didn't have a clue!

***

Two miles up the road at the back door of the industrial strip mall, Eddie rapped on the door bathed in sunshine and smudge.

Knockety-knock-knock. She mimicked the first part of the 'Shave and a Haircut' tune from Roger Rabbit.

A moment later, a sharp *knock-knock* reply was returned, as if a stick or cane was used on the steel door rather than knuckles. Eddie opened the unlocked door and grinned. Winifred was sitting on her scooter, waiting for her, the black plastic ladle she had used to answer the rap in her hand like a scepter. "What took you so long?" she asked.

Eddie shrugged. "A little mix up on who had which instructions. Right now, the ladies are wallpapering downtown and midtown with copies of the posters Rita created. Those were cute." She chuckled. "A pig. Yeah, I'm pretty sure De Luca is doubly insulted. I'm not sure which was worse to him – being portrayed as a mucky farm animal or a cop."

"That's what I was thinking, too," Winifred said. "I'm pretty sure he still thinks of officers of the law as pigs. But wait… You said the ladies were in town. You didn't send Louie, too, did you?"

“No… He didn’t get a chance with the protests from Rita and the others. Is there a reason *you* didn’t want him there?”

“Yes, there is, but if he didn’t go, it doesn’t make a difference. I need to talk to him, though.”

Eddie shook her head. “I think it would be best if you stayed put, too. I don’t think he’s on anyone’s radar, but the less traffic in and out of here, the better. Can you do a video chat?”

Winifred waved away the comment, like his physical presence wasn’t needed. “I’ll call him. I take it you found Lily.”

“The twins did.” Eddie chuckled. “And here I thought those ladies spent too much time on that LOST fan site. Turns out, that’s a great place to send and receive cryptic messages.”

“Will wonders never cease,” Winifred said. “And speaking of wonders, I need to give you the basics on this drone.” She looked to the metal contraption painted with a drab tan and brown camo pattern, a black base beneath it.

“Is that the new ledger?” Eddie asked, pointing to a black book secured to its bottom with spring-loaded clips.

“A perfect reproduction of the original…which will be given to the proper authorities as soon as we can come out of hiding.” She paused and added, “Or at least, most of us.”

Eddie knew not to pursue who ‘most of us’ meant and instead asked about the drone. “So, what makes this different than the ones I used in the service?”

“I tweaked a few things.” Winifred held her smartphone like a microphone. “Otto, I need ambient summer noises at level two.”

A soothing symphony of wind rustling through leaves and evergreen needles, creeks bubbling over rocks, and birds tweeting seemed to be coming from everywhere. “Good grief! It sounds like I’m down at the inlet.”

“Actually, that’s where I had Otto record the sounds. He can also project holograph images. I’d show you now, but I don’t want to use up the battery. Hopefully, Louie knows a good launching site. His information is dated, but animals like De Luca have patterns they're loathed to break. Let me get Louie on the line. I'll need you to take Otto into town."

"No reason to have him suck up battery life when I can pop in, drop him off, and check on our caped crusaders at the same time, right?"

"You always were the brightest wrench in the toolbox, Edna."

"Eddie," she reminded her former teacher. "And by what you've shown and told me about Otto, you've been polishing up your tools, too."

"The thirst for learning and innovating," Winifred said, "may they never disappear or wane."

Chapter 17

"Alphabetize videos and books," Louie typed in. "Oh, and the pantry. Sort the cans into fruit, vegetable, meat, or soup first, then alphabetize. Geez! In the time it takes to have my list finished, I could have done half of these. Hey! I can add organize your closets to this. I already have ours and Lulu's done, but I'll bet some folks don't put shirts and slacks in different areas or colorized from white to pink to red…"

Louie was finally getting into his writing when a loud air horn blasted. He looked around the room and saw it came from his smartphone on the counter. "Hey, that battery was dead when I plugged it into the charger. And I didn't turn it back on."

He picked it up and the horn blasted again. Startled, he tossed it in the air. Hands slapping and grabbing everywhere, he fumbled to catch it before it hit the floor. Finally in control, he powered it on and answered with a harsh, "Knock it off, Winifred!"

"How'd you know it was me?" she tittered, then composed herself. "Never mind, just put me on video phone."

"If you're so smart, do it yourself," Louie said, red-faced at being so frightened by a noise.

Blink!

"There, is that better?" she asked, her smug smirk as irritating as the loud sound had been.

"No, you're still obnoxious. Now that you've taken five years off my life and grayed my hair, what do you want?"

"Is the apartment Luca is in now the same one your…"

Louie cut her off before she could finish. "Yes, Lardo is living in Alonzo's old condo. It's sort of the royal residence of the man in charge of Alaska operations. Or so they brag."

Winifred grimaced, the moment of levity – shocking Louie by accessing his phone when it was off and crowing her accomplishment with the most annoying noise she had found to date – was over. It was time to get down to business. The clock was ticking.

“Is there a weakness in its defenses?”

Louie snorted. “Yeah. Lardo. Luca De Luca the Second makes me look like a rocket scientist or brain surgeon. He doesn’t even have street smarts. His mother claimed ‘the Second’ after his name. He may have looked like his father, but since he didn’t have a dime’s worth of common sense, the old man wouldn’t let him be a junior.”

“I thought that was because Luca the First wanted another son and was saving that designation for him.”

“Well, that isn’t going to happen now, is it?” Louie said with a chuckle. “Last I heard, only men were in that federal prison. He won’t be making any little De Luca’s while he’s in there.”

“Okay. So, do you know if the security at the condo has been updated since he moved in?”

“I wasn’t around when he took over. From what I know of him, though, he probably just changed the décor, not the security. Alonzo was always bragging about how safe his place was. Since he was busted without anyone accessing it, why should it be changed? I’m pretty sure I wouldn’t if it were me.”

Louie paused, noticing LuLu’s bib hanging over the back of her booster seat. “No, I would have, but I don’t think he’d do much more than enlarge the liquor cabinet and change that lock.”

“Well, we’re in luck then, Luck…Louie.” She caught herself before calling him Lucky and began again. “I have the plans for that place, access codes for doors and windows, and with a little bit of palm grease, I can rent a little floor space in the warehouse across the street.”

“So, do you need my help or not? Or was scaring the piss out of me enough?”

“I’m sorry, sort of, for the fright. You have to admit, though, that if you were outside when I called, it would have got your attention."

"It would have got my attention if I was on a milk run to the mini-market two miles away," he said harshly. "Unless you need something else, I'm signing off. I have a project of my own. And if you need me again, try personalizing your ring tone with that Michael Jackson hit. I'll know who it is without you terrorizing the neighborhood."

"You mean 'Thriller'?"

"No. I mean 'Bad.' Goodbye." Louie turned the phone face down on the counter. Even if she could access it, she'd only see *faux* granite. Hanging up on a woman had never been so sweet.

***

Eddie looked over her shoulder at the two devices in the back of her Outback SUV. Winifred's drone was small but sure to be noticed in the relatively empty airspace of downtown Anchorage.

The short side trip she made to her apartment to pick up her own drone was the solution. No need to rent a spot to launch Otto from now. Stealth was great, but two drones – Otto and Eddie II, playing tag in plain sight – was much safer.

A few minutes later, she was at her destination. "Two little birdies flying in the air. One flew off and went down there," she sing-songed softly as she set up both drones.

The first time she had used the Eddie II drone, she decided the traditional game box controller it came with needed modifying. A few clips and snips on an old waterproof phone case, a couple of zip ties to attach it to the back of the controller, and she had created a 'purse' for her phone and could go flying, taking just one compact package with her. That Winifred's genius-drone was controlled by a smartphone app and didn't need a separate device made this venture even more exciting. Distract with one flying machine, accomplish the mission with the other, and still have a way to order pizza when she was done.

***

Ping looked out the window of his captor's rooftop condo. How many times did he have to tell that idiot De Luca he didn't know where that crazy woman was? He had told Zumu many times not to tease or torment customers, especially the local crime lord. No, she had to quietly pick on the man, her anger at all gangsters and thugs focused on the one closest to her at the time.

He looked at the clock. De Luca said the 'specialist' was due in on the midnight flight from Seattle – he would make him talk. Ping shuddered, looking at the roll of plastic that had been brought it. 'Can't mess up the boss's TV room,' Brutus had said. "Hmph!"

Ping studied the digital lock on the window. Even if he knew the combination, it was a thirteen-story drop.

Click.

The door opened and the new man who had been hanging around Brutus came in. He sneered, one lip up like a cut-rate Elvis impersonator. "Time to scoot. Don't talk to anyone on your way out. If they ask, tell them Boss's changed his mind. You're making a run for potstickers and some of that special sauce."

Ping's jaw dropped and his eyes widened.

"I said, scoot!" Zero repeated in a deep, husky growl.

Ping nodded and backed away, bumping into the door frame on his way out. "Oops. Sorry. Oh, and thank you."

Zero mimed zipping his lips.

Ping imitated the gesture, nodded again, and rushed down the hall, shoulders hunched and head down as he tried to be as inconspicuous as possible.

Zero looked out the window and saw two drones playing tag in the sky. A twitch of a smile began and was quickly stifled. *Not yet, Zandra. Not yet.*

***

Brutus looked out at the summer sky from his bed. He'd rather all the windows were covered with blackout curtains at this time of year, but not today. Yes, today he was glad he let her decorate this room the way she wanted. He watched her turn in her sleep, her buxom body bathed in gentle sunlight. All his. He didn't want to admit to the guys he was still head over heels in love with her after ten years, but he was. They didn't even know he had married her. After a bit of bedroom celebrating, the champagne bottle empty on the floor where he'd dropped it after…

"Come back to bed, sweetheart," she called, breaking his reverie. "I want to snuggle."

As trite and cliché as that phrase was, he enjoyed cuddling, too. "Happy anniversary," he whispered. "We can still go out for dinner and drinks if you want, you know."

She opened one eye and saw movement outside. Two UFOs were playing tag, hovering over one another, then racing away. "Damn kids and their drones," she huffed. "Close the curtains, would you? We can open another bottle of Dom for dinner."

***

Ringgg. Ringgg.

Drowsy and still drunk from the champagne they had for dinner, Mrs. Brutus rolled over and flipped open the phone, "I told you never to…"

"Hey, sis. Get out. Now! Take that lame-o husband of yours, too. That is, if you want him to live. Otherwise, leave him there and skip getting a divorce."

"Nick? Is that you?" she whispered as she stumbled out of bed and into the bathroom.

"Yeah, how many other brothers do you have? Look, I'll skip to the short version. De Luca's been outed. The guys got his ledger and found out how bad he's been cheating everyone. He and his A-team are going down. You don't want to be nearby when that happens."

"Got it. Oh, and thanks for the warning."

Click.

"Where'd you get that phone?" Brutus hollered. "I told you…"

"I know, I know, but it's a burn phone and only my brother has the number. He said our world is exploding in minutes, so go now if we want to live."

Brutus popped out of bed like he was spring-loaded. He yanked open the closet door so hard, it popped off its hinges. "Come on! I got the go bag."

She smirked as she pulled out their emergency gear from the ottoman at the foot of their bed. "I think you'd better get dressed first."

He looked down and saw he was naked. "Grrr…" He grabbed the pants, stepped in, and mumbled, "That's another reason I keep you around."

"What's the first?" she asked as she donned her clothes.

"Other than I love you? You always keep a cool head when this happens."

"Yeah, well, now it's time to play the game my way. Passports are in the bag. The next plane leaving to a foreign country, we're on it."

He pulled the UAA sweatshirt over his head and slipped his bare feet into his untied cross-trainers. As soon as her head popped out of the neck of her look-alike sweatshirt, he kissed her on the cheek. "Done deal, doll."

***

Thunk! Thunk! Thunk!

Startled by the pounding on the door, Luca dropped his forkful of pasta in his lap. "Son of a… Hey, somebody get the door."

Somebody wasn't there, though.

Other than the new chauffeur, waiting downstairs in the car, he was alone.

He didn't know it, but everyone on his staff from his bodyguard to his cook had fled at the warning. Nick the Stick wasn't in their organization, but he had a reputation in Anchorage. If he called it, it would happen. Whether he really was a seer or just had incredible inside information, he was both revered and feared at the same time.

Nicholai had made his phone calls soon after he found the ledger. Now it was time for payback. Luca had turned him down for a position in his organization. He hadn't even asked for a top one. Getting in on the bottom floor would have worked. 'We don't want no kraut-sucking commies,' Luca had said.

Nick scoffed as he closed his phone, his last warning given. De Luca didn't know the difference between a German and a Russian, much less a Ukrainian. "Who'd want to work for someone as dumb as you, Lardo? I'll let your enemies clean house, then I'll step in and organize it the way I want."

He scrolled down the pages in the ledger. "Nice forgery – and great timing, whoever sent it – but I would have taken over, even without it."

***

De Luca huffed. What a crappy time for his chauffeur to get sick. He hadn't even called in but had sent a text. Damn him. Still, it was fortunate he left the phone number for a replacement driver. Lucky for him or he would have been driving with two less fingers when he did make it back to work.

The new man arrived moments after he sent the text. He was dim – didn't know to wait downstairs with the car and had pounded on the door, interrupting his meal – but he'd have to do. That he was dark-haired was in his favor. He wouldn't consider himself prejudiced, but as long as his employees were white males with dark hair, they'd work. He shuddered as he thought of the new player in town. Tall, thin, and with greasy blond hair slicked back into a tight queue, Nick the Stick was one more reason not to trust yellow-haired men.

"There's another one," De Luca shouted to his new driver, pointing to the old woman in a red cape.

"What do you want me to do, Boss? Run her over?"

As De Luca considered his options, a woman in a bright purple cape showed up and pulled the one in red into the office supply store. "No. Did you get a picture of her?"

“Which one?” the driver asked.

“Either one.”

“You wanted pictures?”

“Yes, dammit. Why did you ask which one if you didn’t get any? No, never mind. I wanted photographs to find out who’s putting up these disgusting posters.” De Luca picked up the poster he had snatched from the parking garage and tossed it on the floorboard. “Why did you think we were driving around?”

“Um, I thought you wanted me to find flying pigs or something.”

“They’re pig flyers, not flying pigs, you moron. No, I want to find out who’s doing this. Zero’s going to do the erasing.”

“Oh…” The driver leaned forward and smirked. De Luca couldn’t see his face in the mirror when he was this far forward. A little cruising around in the active parts of town to keep the boss away from his condo and irritate him further was just what Jess had asked him to do. Playing dumb was the bonus Arlie gave himself for being called in while on vacation. Hopefully, the black hair dye was temporary. He’d have to ask Louie about that.

***

Still on the tarmac, Brutus looked out the window of the airplane. “Well, would you look at that,” he said and leaned back so his wife could see.

“Who’s that?” she asked.

“Lardo – I mean, De Luca’s – accountant.”

“Are you sure? That man looks like he’s wearing a baggage handler’s uniform.”

“Keep watching…”

“Really? Good grief! He’s wedging himself underneath there. Do you think we ought to tell someone? Won’t he freeze to death in the belly of a plane?”

Brutus sat forward and looked again. “Nah, that’s probably pressurized and heated. See, he’s between two dog crates. I don’t think he picked his plane very well, though. Look.”

“Icelandair. Well, maybe they go to someplace warm.”

"Hmph. I hope that flight's going to northern Siberia!" Brutus said. "There's no love lost between us, that's for sure. He's the one who kicked me out of the easy chair of bookkeeping and wire fraud, tossing me to the curb to handle De Luca's dirty work."

She kissed him on the cheek. "Don't worry, sweetheart. I'm sure you've tucked away enough money to keep us in champagne and cheesecake for the rest of our lives."

"You got that right, doll. *Au revoir*, Alaska!"

"And *Bonjour,* Paris!"

***

"Wha…What are we doing here?" De Luca gasped.

"Well," Arlie turned around in the driver's seat to face him. Dramatically, he took off his chauffeur hat, tore off the big, bushy *faux* mustache, and said without a trace of dimwitted accent, "I figured I'd give you a choice. I can either let you out here in front of the federal building, free to roam without car keys or protection, bait for one of your angry contractors or Nick the Stick. Or I can escort you into the secure entrance. Maybe you and a few of my friend's cohorts can do a little chatting. You know, turn state's evidence in exchange for a little relocation with a new identity."

"That's not much choice: a quick death by dismemberment or a slow one by flipping burgers in Dimweed, South Dakota."

"Ah, but it is a choice." Arlie ran his fingers through his slicked-back hair, trying to get volume in it and the smell of olive oil out. "That's more than you gave Alexander Zokov and Ping."

"Big Z? Oh, yeah, him. That was about ten years ago and my old man, not me. But I…I didn't do anything to Ping! He's up at my condo, kicked back and watching TV. Without cable. And all the doors and windows locked. I was just trying to scare him into telling me where that hostess was. I wanted to know for sure whether she was dead or not."

"Why did you think she was dead? Was it just wishful thinking or something else?"

"Yeah. Yeah, wishful thinking. She…she…she was a real pain. Yeah, I liked the food there at Ping's, but she was…" De Luca stopped talking but his hands kept flapping like his gesticulations meant something.

"Spit it out. Use your words," Arlie said, hoping the mystery of why anyone would want to kill Louie's friend Lily would finally be solved.

"She was disrespectful, that's what."

Arlie shook his head. "You have to be shitting me! Disrespectful? You had a sweet little old woman killed for being disrespectful? You're the one who's disrespectful!"

A sneer sneaked in to overtake De Luca's wince of fear. "You can't blame me for that murder, though, can you? No body, no crime, right?"

Arlie chuckled. "How would you know? Well, you did just admit you had a contract out on her. Whether she was killed or not, whether there's a body or not, you still had intent. I could use this recording as evidence," Arlie held up his phone, indicating he'd recorded their conversation, "and we'd have enough to keep you in prison for the rest of your life. Or tucked away in Dimweed, South Dakota."

"Either way, it's life in prison," De Luca groaned.

"Your choice, Lardo: fast death or slow death."

"Take me in, Arlie. Too bad Uncle Alonzo was a lousy shot. You should have been out of the picture years ago."

"Well, maybe I was destined to stick around so I could take you down, too. Comb your hair. I'm taking you in for pictures and a very long deposition."

***

"Finito," Eddie said flatly into the phone.

"Already?" Winifred asked.

"Yup."

Winifred started to ask more, then realized every word spoken was a chance at being caught by sheer dumb luck. Her one-word reply summed it all up. "Bingo."

Chapter 18

Friday night
Senior Center Bingo Event

"Hey, Eddie, long time no see," Jess said, hand out to shake hers.

Eddie shook it, then stepped back and shrugged. "Yeah, well, Quantico and the FBI really weren't for me. I don't want to be tied down to one place or job."

"Freelancing for the good guys works for you. Not many can pull it off."

"Being a middle-aged woman helps," she said.

"Being smart, fit, and adaptable is more like it. Age is a number. Experience is the quantum theory that solves the problem."

Eddie allowed a grin to escape. She looked up and saw a familiar face. "Hey, Tina! I didn't know you hung out this far south. Village life too boring or are you slumming?"

"Nope. I'm living the high life, working in the big city of Anchorage. Oh, here. I don't think you've met my fiancée, Rita."

"Hey, Eddie," Rita said. "I didn't know you knew Tina."

"I'm full of surprises." Eddie paused and looked away. Spotting someone she knew, a grin spread so wide, her dimples showed.

From across the room, Louie saw Eddie watching him and nodded in acknowledgment.

Jess turned around to see who was making his former FBI partner so happy. A guy or a gal? No one knew her preference, although no one cared, either.

"Louie?" Jess turned to her. "Are you flirting with my fiancé?"

"Your fiancé?" She laughed out loud, a sound that rarely

crossed her lips. “You’re the one full of surprises, Jess. Fiancé?”

Louie walked over to them. “Yes, we’re getting married,” he said, his chin out. “What’s so funny about that?”

“Not a thing. Geez, Louie, I think you got yourself a great partner. Or husband. Either way, congratulations to both of you.”

“Getting married?” Arlie asked.

“Yeah, I popped the question about a week ago,” Jess said. “That’s one reason I asked for your help. I can’t become a widower before I’m married.”

“What are you doing here, Arlie, hanging out at the senior center on bingo night?” Louie asked. He looked up at Arlie’s coal-black hair. “And I think the dye you used is permanent. If I were you, I’d either shave it off or bleach it so you can bring it back to red.”

“Charlene already said she’d give me a buzz cut in the morning. I just wanted one more night to be…ahem…someone else.” Arlie lifted his lip in a sneer. “Thank you. Thank you very much,” he said with an impressive Elvis impersonation.

“Hey, that’s my line,” Zandra said, walking up to the group like she knew everyone.

“Excuse me,” Rita said. “We haven’t been introduced, but you seem familiar.”

Zandra gave the curled upper lip and grunted the same line. “Thank you, thank you very much.”

“Zero? You’re a woman?” Rita asked.

“Who’s Zero?” Louie echoed. “I think I missed something.”

“No, you didn’t,” Zandra said. “From what I understand, you were the beginning of all this. You weren’t meant to see me ‘kill’ Lily.”

“Except it was Hana, right?” Louie asked.

Hana and a young man and woman escorted the shuffling Lily over to the group. “We all safe for now,” the older woman said, waving her hand in the air. “My grandchildren help, too. Maybe they get capes.”

“I’m Joe,” the young Asian American with the shaved head

said to the group. "Oh, and I helped by staying out of the way."

Jennifer stepped forward and introduced herself, then turned to her former teacher. "I recognize a few people here but..." She shook her head, amazed. "Miss Z, I never knew you rode. You were absolutely *awesome* as Zero."

"Thanks. And good job on the fake accent, Jennifer," Zandra said. "I almost didn't recognize you."

"I teach her English," Lily said.

"Yes, you did, Zumu," Jennifer said, giving her a gentle squeeze across the shoulders. "Joe and I both learned many things from you."

"This plan big success," Lily said, one arm out to indicate their little corner of the senior center multipurpose room. "Everyone help, even Detective Arlie come home early from vacation to help protect our town."

"It's a city," Hana whispered in her aunt's ear.

"City, schmitty. Crime still come in where there is vacuum. Crazy ladies in capes still needed." She grinned broadly. "And I want silver one."

Winifred listened from her spot by the window, monitoring two different conversations with her 'hearing aids.' On noticing that Lily wanted to be more actively involved, she pulled up to the group.

"For you, Lily, I think platinum is more your color." She pulled a white tissue-wrapped package out of the basket of her ruby-red motorized scooter.

"Put it on. It's time for your debut, sweetheart," Winifred said sweetly. "Thanks for volunteering to be the sandals on the sidewalk. We couldn't have done it without you."

The men and women on the team gathered around Lily as she tore open the package. "Here, let me help you," Louie said. He shook out the cape and showed it to her first, then to the group, before settling it across her shoulders.

"You know, there were a lot of people involved in taking down the De Luca's," Louie continued, "but none of it would have happened if it weren't for you, Lily. Thank you. Oh, and I think you need to start bringing your fortune cookies out here to bingo night. You could make a killing selling them."

"No killing but selling okay. I no go far. I moved in here yesterday. This is my new home. I donate fortune cookies to fun raiser."

"I think that's *fund* raiser," Louie whispered.

"No, fun raiser. We have fun making up fortunes. That your new job, Mr. Writer."

"Cool! Two writing jobs in one week."

"What's your other one?" Arlie asked.

"I'm writing a book. Bingo, Buzzards, and Bad Boys: Secrets at the Senior Center, a Cozy Mystery for All Ages."

"Wow, that's a mouthful," Rita said. "But I like it." She paused and asked, "It is a fiction story, right?"

Louie chuckled. "Based on a true story. Names and places have been changed to protect the innocent," he said dryly.

Jess patted him on the back. "Amen to that, darlin'. Amen."

Watch for more action with Louie, Rita, Jess, Tina, and all those wily women who want to make the world a better place: CRAZY LADIES IN CAPES: ACT TWO!

If you want to know more about Louie and Rita, the story begins with the Arlie Undercover, a 'Cozy Romantic Suspense' series.

Thank you!

Thank you for reading this cozy mystery spinoff of the Arlie Undercover series. Now that the Crazy Ladies in Capes have a taste of adventure, they'll be back for more. Who knows, maybe Nick the Stick will prove a worthy adversary?

If you could, please take a moment to write a short review, letting others know what you liked about this story. I'd appreciate it, as will others who see what drew you into the story.

More Books by Dani Haviland

THE FAIRIES SAGA SERIES

(Historical fiction/time travel, listed in order):

Kibbles and Bits: ***FREE*** ebook: Sample the early stories in The Fairies Saga stories with extended excerpts and also find out how they got their crazy names.

LOST: The Time Travel Romance That Started It All: (Book One) ***FREE*** eBook! The fun introduction to some of the very colorful characters from The Fairies Saga and Arlie Undercover. Find out how they're influenced by the fan-obsessive romance novel LOST by Lisa Sinclaire.

Naked in the Winter Wind: (Book Two) How does an older woman wind up as a young hottie in Revolutionary War era North Carolina?

Ha'Penny Jenny: (Book Three) More about the naïve and psychic young girl who was adopted into a time traveling family. Will her past catch up to her?

Aye, I am a Fairy: (Book Four) Young British lord finds himself entwined with a time traveling family and must decide if he should go back in time, too.

Dances Naked: (Book Five) Directionally challenged time traveler is rescued by Cherokee in 18th century. What must he do before the chief will show him to The Trees, the portal through time?

Chasing Christmas: (Book Six) A young Cherokee is rescued from an abusive man and changes the lives of many in this 18th century America family.

The Great Big Fairy: (Book Seven) Very tall Benji grew up in the 20th century but was born in the 18th. When he finds a way to return to his grandparents in the distant past, he goes for it. Once there, he realizes he can't stay, but must return to the future.

Little Bear and the Ladies: (Book Eight) What's a bachelor trapper to do with all the females he rescues from the Hessian mercenaries? He'd better hurry and figure something!
Little Drummer Boy: (Book Nine) Young Scout works to earn money for a home in post-Revolutionary War America but runs up against prejudices and snowstorms.
Never Too Young: (Book Ten) Scout and Ha'Penny Jenny have grown up, but will they be able to spend their life together, or will the past and ruffians get in their way?
Time in a Little Blue Bottle**:** (Book Eleven) Elvis, Mark Twain, and the prime vampire are racing to get the bottle of Fountain of Youth water before sweet Bella and the youthful pickpocket. So why are time travelers Marty Melbourne and Master Simon interested?
Kidnapped! (Book Twelve) The Scottish police officer would do anything to get his wife back...even trust the mysterious letter sent to him from his ancestor, a convict on The First Fleet into Australia!
Big Mac: (Book Thirteen) Fate and science said they should never have met but after that first touch, he knew he'd stay with her forever. Would the sudden appearance of the father he never knew be their doom – and the start of a pandemic?

BENJI THE LOST YEARS –

Featuring Benji of THE FAIRIES SAGA

Pool Boy Wanted: No Experience Preferred: (rather racy) Young Benji has been a hostage and slave, but life gets worse when an older woman decides she wants him as her own.
Luke the Unexpected: Love of classic motorcycles brought them together, but Luke and Holly have other challenges to face. Find out how their friend Benji got his stripes here.

TRIPLETS: THREE AREN'T ONE

(A potpourri of literary styles, all with strong characters)

The Set Up**:** Grace's story. A gritty Women's Fiction of how it all began.

Diamonds Aren't for Everyone: Vickie's story. A Billionaire Romance with mysteries and surprises.

That Magic Touch: Ria's story. A tender, heartwarming Medical Romance.

How Love Grows: Tori's story. A spunky young woman insists on doing everything her way. A Romantic Comedy.

They Call Me Sherlock: Silas's story. A young couple who met at Woodstock get a second chance due to creative use of time travel. Romantic Comedy.

ARLIE UNDERCOVER SERIES

(Romantic suspense based in Alaska and Arizona)

A Stingray Christmas: (Book One) Anchorage detective on medical leave travels from Alaska to Arizona to see for the first time the son he'd fathered as an anonymous sperm donor. Great and rotten surprises await the cop with the smartest smartphone around.

The Biggest Heart Ever: (Book Two) When would Arlie learn that trying to do everything by himself could be deadly—and make Charlene a widow before they were married?

Always a Bigger Fish: (Book Three) Back in Alaska, Arlie finds out he's a target. Will vacationing detective Billy Burke (from THE FAIRIES SAGA) have information to help nab the scalper?

How to Fix a Broken Life**:** (Book Four) When Arlie's very pregnant wife is kidnapped by pseudo terrorists, will he be the one to rescue her or will a surprise hero come in to save the day?

Because You Said So: (Book Five) Something's amiss at the Port of Anchorage. Will Arlie be able to solve it and still be back in time to wear the Santa suit?

Heaven and Heartbreak (Book Six) Sharing her child with a gay father and his lover was the easy part. Finding a woman for herself seemed impossible.

THAT TWIN THING SERIES

(Romantic suspense series)

The Midwife's Son: The midwife refused her selfish patient's request to smother the scrawny twin and instead took him home to bring up as her own. Years later, will the two young men wind up in each other's lives despite the midwife's efforts to keep them apart?

Phoenix I'm Not: Will the billionaire's spoiled son be resurrected from the ashes of his former life of drugs and mayhem by love or be tortured and eliminated by the assassin sent by his mother?

Lost and Found Family: Separated at birth, these twins find they have more than genetics in common: they're both the target of killers who are willing to risk everything to take them out.

Peter Elph: A supplement to the story of Lost and Found Family, this short story is about a member of the Wagner family back in 1886 Tombstone, Arizona.

That Twin Thing: The Complete Collection: All four books in one place.

STAND ALONE NOVELLAS

(Contemporary romances)

Kit Kringle: An Alaskan Tale**:** Kay moved to Alaska for the wrong reasons, then decided to stay and start her own business. What she hadn't planned on were prejudices and falling in love.

Be My Angel: Wyatt's dream to help save the wild mustangs began with the purchase of a rundown ranch in western Oregon. What he hadn't anticipated was being mesmerized by a sassy woman in a wheelchair.

Three Are One: The post chaplain tried to help the young widow adjust, but would his feelings for her and the search for his lost sister cause problems?

One Arctic Summer: That unforgettable summer of 1994 in Barrow, Alaska, and the touch she never forgot…If she goes back, will he remember her?

The Polar Xpress: Will the California chiropractor get a first chance at romance with the owner of Second Chance Kennels when he is stranded in Alaska?

Too Fast For You: Ten years after Little League, two talented professional baseball players wind up on the same minor league team. Will she remember him? And will their friendship be ruined if she does?

A Plate of Christmas Cookies: World War Two got between them the first time. Will his adult children stop his second chance at happiness? Based on a true story.

About the Author

Author Dani Haviland started writing late in life and has been making up for lost time with a flood of works from sports, gritty women's fiction, time travel, and Sweet and Sassy romances to Unforgettable romantic suspense, Cute But Crazy rom-coms, and cozy mystery stories – with some short stories thrown in to round out the reading experience.

Dani is also the owner of Chill Out! Books, one of the publishers for The Authors' Billboard. Follow her on BookBub (http://bit.ly/bbdani) to make sure you get her latest stories.

Contact information:
Website: www.danihaviland.com
Email: dani@danihaviland.com
Twitter: @dani_haviland, @gr8authors

I love to hear from readers!

Sign up for my newsletter to get the latest information on new releases, free stuff, and contests here: http://bit.ly/2dhnews

Awesome readers group!

I have a Facebook Page for folks who are interested in early excerpts and insights into my latest books and box sets plus the latest from some of the authors and box sets I publish under Chill Out! Books. I'd appreciate it if you'd like the page. Drop in and see if I've remembered to add photos and excerpts of my works in proccss. Dani Haviland & Friends Readers Group.

www.ingramcontent.com/pod-product-compliance
Lightning Source LLC
Chambersburg PA
CBHW061241170626
46809CB00007B/2778

* 9 7 8 1 9 5 0 5 9 2 3 1 9 *